UMO

A CHILLING TALE OF FIRST CONTACT

A NOVELLA BY

K. PATRICK DONOGHUE

Published by Leaping Leopard Enterprises, LLC

This book is a work of fiction. All the characters, incidents and dialogue are drawn from the author's imagination or are used fictitiously. Any resemblance to actual locations, events or persons, living or dead, is entirely coincidental.

Published by Leaping Leopard Enterprises, LLC
www.leapingleopard.com

First print edition: July 2020
Cover design by K. Patrick Donoghue and Keith Draws
Cover illustration created by and licensed from Keith Draws
Print edition interior design by Amber Colleran
09282021

CONTENTS

Prologue 1

Chapter 1　Black Ops 5

Chapter 2　Mars Approach 13

Chapter 3　Separation Failure 25

Chapter 4　Crossed Wires 33

Chapter 5　First Contact. 47

Chapter 6　Blackout. 59

Chapter 7　Barks And Bites 67

Chapter 8　Take \The Hill. 73

Chapter 9　Baiting The Beast. 79

Chapter 10　For The Greater Good. 89

Chapter 11　Abandoned 97

Epilogue. 99

Bonus: Skywave Prologue 105

About The Author 115

ACKNOWLEDGMENTS

A special mention of thanks to my editor, Katherine Pickett of POP Editorial Services, LLC, and copyeditors Cheryl Hollenbeck and Lisa Weinberg, for their collective help in the creation of *UMO*.

NOTES TO READERS

Greetings, friends, fans and new readers! Thank you in advance for choosing to read *UMO*, the novella prequel to *Skywave*, the first book in my new sci-fi thriller series, the Rorschach Explorer Missions.

The Rorschach Explorer Missions series is my first foray into the realm of science fiction, and readers familiar with my mystery/thriller/suspense series, the Anlon Cully Chronicles, will observe similarities in storyline elements between the two series. I like to blend mystery, alternative history, fantasy and suspense-twists into my plots, and *UMO* is no exception.

I conceived the *UMO* story while writing Skywave and decided to separate it into a stand-alone novella because it didn't fit well in *Skywave*'s timeline, but I liked the story too much to scrap it. While it isn't necessary to read *UMO* to understand the *Skywave* story, or vice versa, *UMO* does provide a deep dive into a backstory referenced at various points in *Skywave*. As an aside, the Prologue for *Skywave* is included in *UMO* as a bonus chapter after the *UMO* Epilogue.

The term UMO is an acronym for unidentified magnetic object, an unexplained phenomenon observed by astronauts and spacecraft cameras since mankind first "slipped the surly bonds of Earth." In my story, UMOs are small, bright lights that travel at supersonic speed near the edges of Earth's atmosphere. They appear capable of non-ballistic motion and seem attracted to spacecraft of all kinds.

Space exploration authorities have, at various times, provided alternative explanations for these bright lights: melting frost shed by spacecraft caught in sunlight, solar wind particles or flaming meteors bouncing off the Earth's atmosphere, to name a few. Conspiracy theorists have suggested the bright lights are an alien life-form visiting our lonely planet. Some have even claimed space exploration authorities have been suppressing the truth about the mysterious lights, a stance they say is reinforced by sudden cuts in video feeds every time one of the bright lights zooms by the cameras of an orbiting spacecraft.

Whom should we believe? The authorities or the contrarians? You be the judge...

P.S. To readers who are astrophysicists, aerospace engineers, astronauts, astronomers, biologists, radio engineers, space agency employees or military members...take it easy on me regarding the leaps of fancy baked into the story. It's fiction. Well, most of it is.

PROLOGUE

n July 1989, the Soviet Union launched two space probes destined for Mars and one of its two moons, Phobos. Dubbed *Phobos-1* and *Phobos-2*, the two spacecraft were armed to the teeth with diagnostic equipment and ambitious objectives.

The early part of *Phobos-1*'s mission was mundane. It was supposed to deploy its array of instrumentation soon after leaving Earth and report back readings of solar and interstellar radiation levels. Once it reached Mars, however, it was to survey the planet and tiny Phobos and then drop a smaller probe onto the moon to drill core samples as a prelude to the arrival of the mission hero, *Phobos-2*.

The latter probe was supposed to study Phobos at much closer range, its mission culminating with the deployment of two smaller probes that would attempt to land on the tumbling clump of rubble and perform more intensive diagnostic assessments.

Neither Phobos probes accomplished their intended missions. *Phobos-1* mysteriously went silent fifty-three days into its two-hundred-day journey to Mars. The Soviets claimed a bad computer command had been sent to *Phobos-1*, triggering a diagnostic program that instructed the probe to turn off its attitude control. In so doing, the probe's solar panels lost their orientation with the sun, causing *Phobos-1*'s batteries to drain instead of recharge. Communication was never reestablished and the probe drifted off into space. It has never been found.

Phobos-2 made it to Mars, but communication with the vessel was inexplicably lost as it approached the final phase of its mission — the deployment of its two landers. Soviet authorities declared the lost communication was attributable to a computer malfunction. The mishap occurred almost nine months after the loss of *Phobos-1*, and like its sister ship, neither *Phobos-2* nor its debris has ever been located.

Enter the United States into this drama. After the successful Viking mission to Mars ended in 1980, the U.S. turned its space exploration focus to other priorities, leaving Mars as an afterthought until the 1992 *Mars Observer* mission. Much like the Soviets' Phobos probes, *Mars Observer* was packed with instruments to examine the Martian atmosphere, climate and magnetic field. And like its ill-fated predecessors, *Mars Observer* failed in its mission.

Three days before it was to insert into orbit around Mars, NASA lost communication with the unmanned spacecraft. As was the case with *Phobos-1* and *Phobos-2*, attempts to reestablish communication were unsuccessful. NASA's explanation for *Mars Observer*'s demise? A fuel leak caused the probe to spin out of control, and much like *Phobos-1*, *Mars Observer*'s solar panels were unable to maintain orientation with the sun, causing the eventual drain of its batteries. Neither *Mars Observer* nor its debris has ever been spotted. It was believed to have drifted off into space like its Soviet counterparts.

CHAPTER 1

BLACK OPS

UNITED STATES SPACE COMMAND
PETERSON AIR FORCE BASE
COLORADO SPRINGS, COLORADO
DATE: 04.27.1995
TIME: 0438 UTC

Eyes glued on his computer screen, Lieutenant General Timothy Ferris scanned the closing of his message to the secretary of defense one last time.

"The time for theories and finesse have passed. We have wasted a year and untold millions of dollars on NASA's boondoggle and we are in no better position today than if we had followed my plan from the get-go. Given the XGEN test results, there is only one plan of action to deal with the UMOs that makes sense. I seek your support to put that plan in front of the president, and the authority to see the plan through to its successful execution."

Ferris clicked the print button and pushed back from his desk. Would SECDEF support him this time? Or would Karen Wells get the better of him, again? NASA's chief administrator was three times the politician the estimable George Wentworth on a bad day. On a good day, she made SECDEF look like a third-grade thumb sucker.

With the printout in hand, Ferris returned to his desk to review it again. It had to be perfect to overcome Wentworth's "get along to get ahead" attitude and Wells' crafty sidesteps. As he read the opening paragraph, Ferris thought aloud, "At least there's no dispute about the facts."

"Phobos-1, Phobos-2 and Mars Observer all met the same fate at the hands of the same foe. A foe that just obliterated our XGEN satellite. A foe that has been at our doorstop from the moment we entered outer space. A foe we are ill-prepared to defeat. Yet, we have the means and opportunity to change our circumstances if we have the courage to act decisively."

Scanning ahead several paragraphs, Ferris made a note on the printout to bold the sections of the CIA interview that spurred him to recommend more drastic measures. He still found it remarkable that the two Soviet scientists, code-named Spud and Nick, had willingly parted with such valuable intelligence.

"Spud stated official versions of CHARIOT-ALPHA and CHARIOT-BETA losses are bogus. Spud claimed both were destroyed by unidentified entities. When asked to clarify what he meant by 'unidentified entities,' Nick produced photographs showing balls of light surrounding CHARIOT-BETA."

Ferris slid a copy of one of the referenced photographs from the black-taped SPUDNICK envelope on his desk. In the grainy image, *Phobos-2*'s camera had captured bright lights gathering around the Soviet probe. As he looked at the photograph, Ferris recalled his reaction when first briefed on the scientists' story. He had glared at the Air Force intelligence officer providing the briefing and said, "What a load of steaming horse shit."

But he had changed his tune after the intelligence officer shared another set of photographs. The pictures showed the demolished remains of *Phobos-1*. The Soviet scientists explained that *Phobos-2* had launched a week after *Phobos-1* from the Baikonur Cosmodrome and had passed through its debris field within days of losing communication with the lead probe.

After reviewing copies of the second set of photographs, Ferris revisited his excerpt of NASA's analysis of the photographs and data supplied by Spud and Nick.

"Instrument readings reveal a significant spike in electromagnetic radiation in Phobos-1's final moments. Taken in conjunction with the photographs, it appears a 'swarm' of the lights generated an electromagnetic pulse, destroying the Soviet probe."

Damn right, they did. No question about that now, Ferris thought.

Turning his attention to the next section of the memo, Ferris decided to strike the CIA memo passages related to the Soviet military's "bad computer command" cover story for the loss of *Phobos-1*. The president, SECDEF and Wells were all familiar with the story by now.

"Spud said military convinced CHARIOT-ALPHA destroyed by U.S. SDI asset. Nick said the last instructions communicated to probe ordered it to activate its instrumentation to begin taking radiation readings. Spud said mili-

tary believes activation of CHARIOT-ALPHA's devices was detected by U.S. asset and said asset neutralized CHAR-IOT-ALPHA to prevent its instruments from detecting the U.S. asset's presence.

"Spud was visibly upset when discussing military theory. Based on photographic and instrumentation evidence, Spud is convinced both CHARIOTS were destroyed by the lights. Nick concurred, saying he believed the lights attacked CHARIOT-BETA in response to the activation of its elec-tromagnetic-radiation detecting instruments, just like they had with CHARIOT-ALPHA."

Ferris circled the last line of the statement and examined the *Phobos-2* picture again. Hundreds of the lights formed a bee-like swarm near the probe's communications array and instrumentation. He murmured, "Damn swarm looks just like the one that took out our XGEN, only bigger."

Skipping past the rest of his documented support, Ferris zeroed in on the crux of the debate between Space Command and NASA.

"For decades, NASA had publicly disavowed the existence of so-called 'unidentified magnetic objects,' despite a grow-ing catalog of videos and astronaut reports of UMO 'fire-flies' flitting around spacecraft and satellites. Even among those in-the-know, NASA persists in its stance that UMOs are benign, inanimate particles trapped in Earth's ionosphere."

Ferris wrote in the margin, "Lies!"

UMOs were neither benign nor inanimate. They were an alien life-form that fed on electromagnetic radiation, and despite NASA's decades-long contention that the UMOs were harmless, the *Phobos-1* and *Phobos-2* photos showed otherwise…as did the XGEN test results.

He decided to bold and underline the thrust of his argument.

"Now that we've seen what they can do firsthand (re: XGEN), what happens if a swarm of these things hits one of our surveillance satellites? Or a nuke guidance satellite? They could leave us blind to attack. Or, worse, what if they take out a Russian satellite? The Russians are bound to think we did it and before you know it, we will have a full-scale nuclear war on our hands! We cannot ignore UMOs any longer! They represent an imminent threat to our national security."

It would be hard, if not impossible, for NASA's chief to disagree with that conclusion now, Ferris thought. Not after the XGEN results. But it didn't mean Wells wouldn't try. She'd probably trot out the same arguments she'd used to send *Mars Observer* to its doom, and the same logic she'd used to secure the president's sanction of the *Cetus Prime* mission.

The problem with *Phobos-2* and *Mars Observer* had been an issue of time, not objective, according to Wells. Given the communication-loop delay between Mars and Earth, both probes had been overwhelmed before anyone knew about it. Her solution? Send a manned mission to Mars.

"What an asinine proposal!" Ferris lamented. "And now look at the mess we're in!"

This time, Ferris prayed, would be different. This time, the president would have to see it his way. No more pussyfooting with the alien creatures. It was time to show them teeth!

As he finished rereading his proposal to that effect, Ferris was left with one open question — would the crew of *Cetus Prime* man up and do what was necessary?

Laying aside the draft to SECDEF, Ferris opened another classified envelope on his desk labeled CETUS. Inside were details of the spacecraft, its mission and crew. Ferris flipped pages until he reached the crew bios.

The commander of the mission was Lieutenant Colonel Avery Lockett. The black Air Force fighter pilot was a decorated veteran, including several covert military operations during the 1980s. He had not aspired to be an astronaut, but Ferris had demanded the selection of an active military officer with combat experience to lead the mission. When presented with the assignment, Avery had been given the chance to decline, but he opted to go, saying it was the opportunity of a lifetime.

The same sentiments had been expressed by the other two members of the skeleton crew, Captain Nick Reed, the flight engineer and copilot, and Mission Specialist, Dr. Christine Baker. Of these two, only Nick was a career astronaut. Though he'd never been into space, Nick had trained for several Shuttle missions and knew the ship's systems, inside and out. Ferris had supported Reed's inclusion more because of his reputation for being cool under pressure than his technical knowledge.

Christine, on the other hand, was a liability in Ferris' mind. Neither a member of the military nor a career astronaut, she had been nominated for the mission by NASA given her expertise in predatory animal behaviors. More at home on the African safari than a laboratory or spaceship, the biologist viewed the mission as a chance to examine the first known alien species rather than an operation to preserve national security. Despite his reservations about her, Ferris had agreed to NASA's choice of Christine in exchange for the space agency's assent to Avery's appointment as commander.

A motley crew, to be sure, Ferris thought. Could they be counted on to do as ordered? Or would it prove necessary to force their compliance?

MARS APPROACH

CETUS PRIME
FLIGHT DECK
DATE: 04.28.1995
TIME: 1200 UTC

very Lockett floated through the hatch and propelled
forward to reach the flight deck ladder. With a gen-
tle tug on a rung, he glided up the length of the ladder and into the cockpit. Grabbing hold of the commander's seat, Avery curled into a ball and guided
his body into place.

After strapping in, Avery paused to gaze at Mars
through the cockpit window. A month ago, the planet had
been little more than an orange pebble against a black
backdrop. But now, only days from inserting into orbit,
Mars dominated the *Horizon* and Avery could see its sur-
face features in vivid detail. He was most impressed by the
sight of Olympus Mons, the planet's massive volcano. Pur-
ported to be the largest volcano in the solar system, the
northern hemisphere behemoth looked like a giant eye
keeping watch over those who approached.

The previous night, Christine Baker had been the first
to spot Phobos as it appeared from behind the planet's

shadow. She'd called Avery and Nick Reed to the lab and together they'd watched the tiny spec zoom around the planet's midsection through a porthole window. Avery had been amazed by the moon's diminutive size and by how close it orbited its host planet. He had been aware of the moon's dimensions and proximity to Mars before the mission jumped off, but the descriptions and pictures didn't do justice to either the disparity in size between the two orbs or Phobos' atmosphere-scraping altitude.

As Avery tried to locate the moon again through the cockpit window, he found it hard to believe a chunk of tumbling rock less than seventeen miles across had been the source of so much trouble. For NASA and the Soviets, Phobos was the Bermuda Triangle of Mars, an analogy that had drawn hisses from Christine when Avery coined the phrase during their porthole viewing.

"This mission is eerie enough without you adding more voodoo to it," she had said, touching her head, heart and shoulders to invoke holy protection.

She had been right to describe their mission as eerie, thought Avery, although she could have attached other adjectives as well. Crazy, dangerous and desperate were three he had come up with during the seven-month journey, but he kept these descriptors to himself. Christine's superstitions had already risen to obsessive-compulsive levels, and he didn't want to encourage any further expansion this close to beginning the important tasks that lay ahead.

Yet, he was concerned about Christine. The freckle-faced redhead now spent hours at her station in the lab, staring at the instrumentation displays, waiting for the first sign of the UMOs to light up her screens. All the while, she tapped her foot and fidgeted with her Chicago Cubs cap.

It was quite a contrast to the nerves-of-steel reputation that preceded Christine's selection for the mission. As Avery had heard it, Christine had once stepped between poachers surrounding a wounded black rhino during a safari expedition, daring them to shoot her. The game hunters had scattered when the fallen animal took advantage of the respite to rise to its feet and signal a charge, leaving Christine alone with the angry beast. She turned to face the rhino as it snarled and huffed, standing her ground during several feigned charges until eventually the animal lost interest and ran off. Thereafter, she was known among her Kenyan guides as *"Tamasha ya Rhino,"* the rhino tamer.

He'd seen flashes of the rhino tamer within Christine during training, but the deeper they traveled in space, the further they flew from their familiar surroundings, the shakier she became. Whether it was fear of the unknown, or a by-product of the long journey, the change in her behavior was so pronounced Avery worried whether she could hold it together long enough to complete their mission.

Turning away from the window, Avery donned a headset and pressed the microphone button. "Rise and shine, folks. Time to get to work."

With their morning system checks completed, the three members of *Cetus Prime*'s crew gathered in the galley for a quick breakfast and briefing. Over granola, dried fruit and pouch-and-straw-served coffee, Avery kicked off the proceedings.

"Okay, first order of business. We need to get our baby birds ready to fly. I want to test-drive all three before we get into orbit," he said.

"Roger that," Nick said. "Let's do *CPO* first. Then *Andromeda*, and save *Perseus* for last."

CPO, or *Cetus Prime Orbiter*, was a small instrumentation probe that would perform long-range scans of their planned orbital path around Mars. It would hunt for debris from *Phobos-2* and NASA's *Mars Observer*. *CPO* would also serve as a sentinel, using its electromagnetic detection devices to provide the *Cetus Prime* crew with an early warning of any UMOs in their path.

Once *CPO* located the wreckage, *Andromeda* would swoop in to examine the debris in detail. *Andromeda*'s payload included telescoping robotic arms the crew would use to gather samples of the wreckage. In addition, the probe was outfitted with cameras to document the debris trail and an X-ray generator to look inside damaged sections deemed too big to fit in *Cetus Prime*'s storage bay.

Andromeda also carried spectrometers similar to those onboard *CPO* to detect sources of electromagnetic radiation in and around the remnants of *Phobos-2* and *Mars Observer.*

Perseus, the third of *Cetus Prime*'s baby birds, would lag behind *CPO* and *Andromeda*. Armed with a dozen missiles fitted with EMP grenades, *Perseus* would maintain a position between the two scientific probes and *Cetus Prime*. At the first sign of trouble from the UMOs, *Perseus* would be activated to protect the mothership.

"Shouldn't we test *Perseus* first?" Christine asked. "Just in case the UMOs show up before we get into orbit."

"Doesn't matter to me, but this far out, I don't think we have anything to worry about," Nick said. "Your call, Commander. I'll send 'em out in any order you want."

Good old Nick, thought Avery. As accommodating as ever. The flight engineer and copilot was as unflappable as astronauts come. Nothing fazed him. Avery had once teased him that if Nick were captain of a plane plunging toward the ground, he would be the guy who'd come on the intercom in a soothing tone and say, "Good afternoon, folks. For those of you seated on the right side of the plane..."

Yet, despite his laid-back attitude, sandy-haired surfer-boy looks and country charm, Nick was the most versatile astronaut Avery had ever met. He could fly the bird, fix the bird and man any of its stations. Hell, he was the bird! His only flaw, so far as Avery could judge, was the odor that enveloped him. Granted, they all reeked at this point, but Nick was monkey-house nasty after seven months in space.

"Let's stick with your plan, Nick," Avery said. "We'll keep *Perseus* deployed for good once we complete the shake-out. No sense in deploying it twice."

"Roger that," Nick said.

Christine lowered her head and stared at the floor with vacant eyes. She mouthed a comment, but Avery couldn't make out what she said. It didn't matter, though; he understood the meaning behind her gestures. She was worried that activating *CPO's* and *Andromeda's* electromagnetic scanners might attract the UMOs, leaving them vulnerable to attack if *Perseus* was still docked. But they weren't close to Phobos yet, nor had they picked up any UMO activity on their approach to Mars, and Avery didn't want to manage the mission based on fear of an absent threat.

"Next item. Any news from Goddard, Chris?" Avery asked.

"Huh?" said the zoned-out Christine.

"Did you get an update on the latest round of MAG-SAT tests in yesterday's uplink?" Avery clarified.

The MAG-SAT tests represented the second arm of NASA's two-pronged approach to determine what had caused the UMOs to destroy *Mars Observer* and the two Soviet probes. While there was a strong conviction within the agency that the attacks had been triggered by the activation of electromagnetic instrumentation aboard the three Martian probes, there was no consensus as to which instrument or combination of instruments had been the catalyst.

In response, NASA had launched experimental satellites to the outer edge of Earth's atmosphere to broadcast different forms of electromagnetic radiation, hoping to lure UMOs to the satellites and stimulate a swarm like the one depicted in photos taken by *Phobos-2*. But, thus far, the MAG-SAT experiments had failed to provide any insights.

From what NASA had shared with Avery during the trip to Mars, the MAG-SAT experiments had been a bust because there were too few of the creatures circulating in Earth's ionosphere, and too many competing sources of radiation from other satellites, terrestrial radio waves and solar wind to attract a critical mass of the UMOs to the MAG-SATs. But NASA continued to tweak the experiments, even as *Cetus Prime* closed in on Mars, hoping for a breakthrough that would provide the crew with intelligence that might help avert an attack.

"Um. No. Still no swarm. Not even a gaggle," Christine said. "In fact, Dr. Braun's beginning to waffle on her theory about the UMOs."

Dr. Heidi Braun was a biologist, like Christine. She had been hired by NASA as a consultant for the Cetus Prime mission because of her research specialty: animal swarming. She had been a leading investigator on the seemingly esoteric subject for more than a decade, studying the swarming behavior of starlings, sardines and honey bees, among other animals.

"Waffling, how?" Nick asked.

"She's always contended the *Phobos-2* photo showed classic signs of migratory swarming," Christine said.

"Right. Because she said it's unusual for swarms to attack," Nick said.

"Exactly. Honey bees, for example, swarm when their hives become overpopulated. The queen of the hive births a new queen and then leaves the hive to establish a new colony, taking thousands of bees with her. They form a swarm around the old queen to protect her from predators while they search for a spot to establish a new hive," Christine said.

Avery recalled the passionate defense Braun had given in favor of the migratory theory. The UMOs hadn't attacked the spacecraft because they posed threats, she had said. They'd attacked them because they were rich in electromagnetic radiation, the theorized food source of the UMOs. Honey bees, Braun had told NASA, often stop at interim points in their hunt for a new home to rest or nourish themselves. She believed the unlucky probes had come across hungry UMO nomads during their search for a new home in the solar system.

She based her theory, in part, on the fact that Mars has a significantly weaker magnetic field than Earth. As Braun had pointed out, Mars' magnetosphere and ionosphere are almost nonexistent, meaning there isn't an abundant source of ions in Mars' atmosphere for the UMOs to feed upon. So, Braun deemed the possibility of a hive or colony of UMOs orbiting Mars unlikely.

NASA had been quick to latch onto Braun's wandering-nomad theory, for it solved a puzzling riddle. Why had these specific probes been attacked, while previous probes sent to Mars had made it to the planet without encountering a swarm of UMOs?

Lastly, Braun posited a final reason in defense of her migratory theory versus the notion of outright predatory behavior, the favored theory of the Pentagon.

"Herds of African antelope swarm when under attack by lions or other safari predators," she had said. "In so doing, the weaker beasts in the herd gravitate to the periphery of the swarm, while the stronger animals aggregate inside the swarm's protective bubble. It's believed to be an evolutionary adaptation. Protect those most likely to propagate the species by sacrificing the weakest to predators. The same behavior has been observed in starling flocks and other animal herds."

She told NASA and the Pentagon that the same behavior applied to migrating honey bees. The queen is considered tantamount to a colony's survival. She is at the very heart of the swarm, with expendable worker bees surrounding her. Presuming the UMOs had evolved a similar hierarchy, Braun had contended, it would go against the survival-of-the-species instinct for the whole swarm to attack. They would want to protect their "queen" or strongest members. The swarm would be more inclined to flee rather than fight.

Avery supposed Braun's wavering commitment to her migratory theory was based on NASA's continued inability to attract a swarm to feed on one of its electromagnetic-radiation-generating satellites. "What's her theory now?"

"She's drifting toward the Pentagon theory," Christine said, her voice weak.

"How long has she been drifting?" Avery asked.

Christine shrugged, still staring at the floor. "I dunno. She's seemed more uptight in her last few messages, but she didn't say anything outright about having second thoughts until yesterday. She didn't say why, but I think the last round of MAG-SAT experiments tipped her over the edge."

"Doesn't surprise me." Nick yawned. "I'm sure Ferris is leaning on her pretty hard."

"Yeah," Christine said. "That, and we haven't run into any UMOs during our trip. I'm sure everybody at NASA is leaning toward the predator theory by now."

There was truth in Christine's and Nick's comments, thought Avery. The military had been steadfast in their conviction that the UMOs had inflicted a surgical assault on *Phobos-1*, based on the damage to the probe evident in *Phobos-2*'s fly-by photographs. *Phobos-1*'s comms array had been sheared off and partially melted. And while not all of the probe's instrumentation could be seen in the pictures, those that were visible had been pierced through with laserlike precision. The same was true of the section housing the spacecraft's nickel-cadmium batteries.

With each failed MAG-SAT test, General Ferris had ratcheted up pressure on NASA to treat the UMOs as hostile entities. This much Avery knew from private messages he'd exchanged with Colonel Paul Morgan, CAPCOM for the Cetus Prime mission. In those messages, Morgan hadn't provided Avery with any indication that Braun was wavering. He'd just said, "Chest-thumping in Arlington can be heard in Greenbelt."

That said, Morgan had to know of Braun's change of heart. As CAPCOM, Morgan was the crew's primary communication conduit with NASA. All communication between Mission Control and *Cetus Prime* passed through Morgan. Therefore, Braun's message to Christine would have received Morgan's review before transmission. Given that, it surprised Avery that Morgan hadn't provided him with a direct heads-up. He would have to ping Morgan after the crew briefing to find out why.

"Whether Braun's wavering or not, it doesn't change anything about our mission," Avery said. "Everybody back home is just guessing, anyway."

"You're wrong, boss," Nick said, covering his mouth to hide another yawn.

"Wrong about what?" Avery asked.

"Braun wavering does change one thing," Nick said.

"Yeah, what's that?"

"I agree with Chris. We should test *Perseus* first."

CHAPTER 3

SEPARATION FAILURE

CETUS PRIME
PALLET CONTROL CENTER
DATE: 04.28.1995
TIME: 1718 UTC

While Nick went aft to prepare to launch *Perseus* from *Cetus Prime*'s pallet, Christine returned to the lab to monitor her bank of instruments. Avery returned to the flight deck and typed a message to transmit to Morgan. It read, "*CDR to CC: Heard the beekeeper is moving to Arlington. Should we be concerned? CDR out.*"

Given Earth and Mars were sixty-five million miles apart at this point in their journey, Avery's message would take six minutes to reach Morgan's console at the Goddard Space Flight Center in Greenbelt, Maryland. Assuming he read the message right away and responded immediately, the quickest Avery could expect a reply was in twelve minutes.

However, Morgan tended to wait for a routine mission update before responding to one of Avery's thinly-coded messages. Avery supposed Morgan did this to avoid attracting undue attention of others in Mission Control who were copied on all ship-to-Earth communications, most notably the mission director, Dennis Pritchard, and Ferris' Space Command duty officer.

Morgan was a straight shooter in Avery's experience, so he expected a candid answer, whenever it came. He was more interested to see Morgan's word choices, for they would reveal how far the pendulum had swung toward the military point of view. If Morgan's message was uncoded, Avery would interpret it to mean there was consensus between NASA and the Pentagon, whatever his answer. If Morgan's reply contained coded language, it would mean there was a battle brewing between the two factions.

"Hey, Commander?" came Nick's query through Avery's headset.

"Yeah, Nick. What's up?"

"Got a problem with *Perseus*. Better get down here and see for yourself."

"On my way," Avery said, unclipping his safety harness.

The trip to reach Nick involved a float down the flight deck access panel to reach the forward fuselage's middeck, where the ship's communications center was located. From there, Avery passed through a hatchway and proceeded through the laboratory, flying by the foot-tapping Christine on the way. At the far end of the lab, he glided through another hatchway and into the compartment housing the crew galley and quarters. After passing through a third and final hatchway, he reached the aft compartment, home of the ship's engine control room and pallet control center.

Avery found Nick peering out the porthole at the pallet beyond the aft compartment. The girderlike structure sat between *Cetus Prime*'s main cabin and the engine compartment at the ship's stern. The engine compartment of the ship also contained the storage bay where the crew would house debris salvaged during their mission. From the side, the pallet looked like a flatbed train car wedged between two boxcars. At the front of the pallet rested the three probes, docked side by side. Behind the probes, the pallet was populated by a variety of antennas and other instruments that protruded in every direction like the spines of an angry porcupine.

When Avery arrived, Nick said, "Damn thing won't separate. I think one of the docking clamps is stuck. All the control panel says is 'sep-fault.'"

"Did you check the hydraulics?" Avery asked.

"Yes sirree. Pressure gauge shows nominal, same with the temp gauge. Actuator seems to be functioning properly. That leaves the clamps. Trouble is, I can't see them. Too dark on the pallet."

Nick moved aside to let Avery look out the porthole. Sure enough, the pallet was obscured by the shadow cast by the ship's dual-wing solar panels.

"I take it the pallet lights aren't working," Avery said.

"You got it. I checked the fuse, it's still good. Bulbs probably froze. It's an easy fix, but it requires an EVA to change out the bulbs," Nick said with a smile. "I can inspect *Perseus* while I'm out."

"Uh-huh," Avery said.

Nick had a thing for extravehicular activity, a.k.a. spacewalking, and for weeks he'd been crowing about his intention to become the first astronaut to perform an EVA in Mars' orbit. He'd even prepared a speech for the occasion, which he'd recited more than two dozen times over crew dinners.

"You know it won't count," Avery said. "We're not in orbit yet."

"I don't know what you're talking about," Nick said. "I'm just trying to get our baby bird airborne."

The earnest expression on Nick's face made Avery laugh. "Nice try."

"What?"

"Look, seriously, is the *Perseus* sep-fault legit or not?" Avery asked.

"One hundred percent legit. I wouldn't mess around with something like that."

Avery stared him down, waiting for a crack in Nick's poker face. When none appeared, Avery said, "Let me roll the ship to get the pallet in the sun, get you a clean look at *Perseus* from inside," Avery said. "If you still can't tell what's going on, we'll suit you up."

"Roger that." Nick grinned.

"Don't get all giddy. There's a condition."

"Condition?"

"Yeah, when you get back inside, take a sponge bath, put on some cologne, change your clothes, man. My eyelashes are going to fall out if you don't deal with your eau-de-whiff."

The roll maneuver illuminated the pallet, but not the cause of *Perseus*' separation-fault error message. So, Avery met Nick at the airlock in the crew compartment to assist Nick into his extravehicular mobility suit, or EMU, and SAFER thruster pack. He then stepped out of the airlock and cranked the inner hatch shut. With the airlock sealed, Nick began the two-hour depressurization process while Avery returned to the cockpit to apprise Mission Control of the situation and their plan. The time was 1752 UTC.

At 1955 UTC, Avery gave Nick the go-ahead to begin the EVA. Nick activated his helmet's solar shield and cranked open the airlock's outer door. Before exiting *Cetus Prime*, he clipped the D-ring of his safety tether to the fuselage handrail and checked the display and control module strapped to his chest to verify the suit's life support and power supply were functioning properly. Once outside *Cetus Prime*, he cranked the airlock closed and glided toward the pallet.

Avery watched Nick's progress via monitors mounted on the cockpit's instrumentation console, while Christine watched from similar monitors in the lab.

As they waited for Nick to change out the frozen light-bulbs, Avery turned his thoughts to *Perseus* and its weapons. He wouldn't admit it to either Christine or Nick, but Avery was convinced the probe's weapon system was more window dressing than lethal firepower.

NASA had no idea whether an EMP charge would kill or injure the UMOs. It was quite possible it would just piss them off. And the damn little space fireflies could move at supersonic speed. Firing one of their missiles at a swarm of them would be like shooting a pop gun at a moving train: one would have to guess their path and fire ahead of it. Unlike a train, however, swarms were capable of changing direction in a heartbeat, whether bees, starlings or electromagnetic alien life-forms.

Still, thought Avery, it was better to have something that might fend off an attack than to face the creatures with no means of defense. And Avery took some comfort in the belief the missiles might provide *Cetus Prime* a means of escape, even if they missed their target.

Each missile carried a lure of sorts, designed to attract and draw the UMOs away from *Cetus Prime* and its cadre of probes by emitting a stream of ions in its wake. Again, the concept was a total swag, but it made sense to Avery. The UMOs fed on ions trapped between Earth's magnetosphere and ionosphere. If the weapon system worked as advertised, the swarm would follow the missile, gobbling up the ions in its trail, until the EMP warhead exploded. If the resulting EMP blast didn't kill them, the Pentagon and NASA hoped it would act like a shock grenade, disorienting them long enough for *Cetus Prime* and its probes to retreat or fire another missile.

But if the missiles proved useless, *Cetus Prime* had no backup weaponry. Their only choice would be to turn and flee, and Avery knew they couldn't outrun the UMOs under normal conditions. He couldn't begin to imagine how fast they might fly if enraged.

"Okay, mission accomplished. Can one of y'all flip the switch in the pallet control room, please," Nick said over the intercom.

"Roger that," Christine said. "I'll take care of it, Commander."

"Copy," Avery said.

Moments later, Christine said, "Switch isn't working."

"Try jiggling the fuse. Might've come loose when I was looking at it," Nick said.

Sure it did, Avery thought.

After a short delay, the pallet lights appeared on Avery's monitor. Nick gave a thumbs-up to the pallet camera and said, "Let there be light. Requesting permission to proceed to *Perseus*."

"Permission granted," Avery said.

At 2011 UTC, Nick arrived at the platform upon which *Perseus* was anchored. While Christine watched him from the pallet porthole, Nick began to examine the probe's docking clamps. At the same moment, the X-ray spectrometer in the laboratory compartment began to record violent spikes.

Out of the black appeared a stream of UMOs...hurtling straight for *Cetus Prime*.

CHAPTER 4

CROSSED WIRES

CETUS PRIME MISSION CONTROL
GODDARD SPACE FLIGHT CENTER
DATE: 04.28.1995
TIME: 1758 UTC

When Colonel Paul Morgan entered the astronaut program as an Air Force captain, his aim had been singular: make it into space. He hadn't cared if it was a rotation on *Skylab*, a Shuttle mission or something more exotic, like a trip to the moon or Mars. In fact, he'd have ridden into orbit strapped to the side of an Atlas rocket, if necessary.

His dream came true in ways he could never have imagined. He'd been to space four times, logging over eight hundred hours beyond Earth's confines. Three Shuttle missions, two of them as flight commander, a rotation on *Skylab* and forty hours of spacewalking made Morgan one of NASA's most decorated astronauts.

Around the halls of NASA's facilities, however, Morgan was revered more for a single, selfless act of bravery than for his illustrious track record. The year was 1989, and Morgan had piloted the Space Shuttle *Horizon* to deploy a classified satellite for the Department of Defense. The mission had gone smoothly until the satellite was released from the Shuttle's cargo bay. With the satellite a safe distance from the Shuttle, an attempt was made to remotely activate the satellite's rocket, which would propel the payload to its intended orbital location.

The rocket did not fire, however, leading to the possible loss of a vital surveillance asset at a time when the Soviet Union was on the brink of collapse and tensions were escalating in the Persian Gulf. A decision was made in Houston to have *Horizon* "catch" the drifting satellite and manually activate its rocket by pulling a lever on the side of the satellite with a makeshift lasso extended from the Shuttle's cargo arm.

It was as dangerous an impromptu work-around as ever contemplated by NASA, for there was a chance the rocket had failed to fire due to an engine fault, rather than a command fault. Activating the engine manually risked an explosion, which would destroy both the satellite and *Horizon*, killing all the astronauts aboard. Further, the lasso had to be weak enough to break free from the cargo arm once the lever was pulled or else the tethered satellite might crash into the Shuttle when its engine ignited.

Two astronauts had performed EVAs to observe the DoD payload's release from the cargo bay, and they remained there as Morgan maneuvered the Shuttle to close the gap with the powerless satellite. Inside *Horizon*, other crew members worked together to construct the makeshift lasso. Once constructed, the astronauts in the Shuttle bay attached it to the cargo arm. They then extended the cargo arm and lasso, but the lasso was too flimsy to hook onto the satellite's engine lever without assistance, so Mission Control instructed one of the astronauts to climb the cargo arm and hand guide the loop of the ten-foot-long plastic lasso over the lever.

At seventeen thousand miles per hour, separated by no more than twenty feet, the two spacecraft flew in tandem. With one arm clutching the cargo arm, Mission Specialist Julia Carillo reached up to take hold of the plastic lasso just as three golf-ball-sized lights zoomed in front of her helmet. Startled, she let go of both the cargo arm and the lasso. "Jesus, what the —"

On the flight deck, Morgan's eyes darted to the cargo bay camera feed. "Repeat, Julia. What's going on?"

The satellite, pulled toward the Shuttle by the magnetic wake created by the illuminated objects, crashed into Carillo, striking her helmet. The satellite began to tumble, knocking her away from the cargo bay.

"Oh, shit!" Morgan said.

"*Horizon*, report," said the voice of CAPCOM in Houston.

As Carillo drifted toward the rear of the Shuttle, her safety tether reached its end. The whip of the taut cable caused her to bounce off one of the cargo bay doors, rendering her unconscious. The other astronaut in the bay, Mission Specialist Benjiro Saito hunkered down to seek cover just as the tumbling satellite clipped the cargo arm, snapping it in two.

"*Horizon*, abort SAT engine start," instructed Houston.

At the same time, chatter erupted from the crew watching the drama unfold from inside the Shuttle. The spacecraft lurched right when the cargo arm snapped, initiating a roll. Morgan looked up to see debris spray past the windows.

"Oh, no," Morgan said.

With only seconds remaining before catastrophe, Morgan went into action. He steadied the roll with quick taps of the thruster controls, then employed stronger bursts of the thrusters to lower and slow the Shuttle, allowing the careening satellite to shoot forward of the ship. As he completed the maneuvers, an ear-splitting scream filled his headset. The flailing portion of the cargo arm still attached to the Shuttle had cut through the unconscious astronaut's tether, knocking her limp body away from the ship.

"Astronaut off-structure!" called one of the crew.

"Get her, Benji! Get her quick!" yelled another.

"*Horizon*, abort. Repeat, abort!" CAPCOM ordered. "Get *Horizon* out of there, Paul."

Saito, still hunkered down in the bay, arrived too late to reach the broken tether. "Damn! Damn! Damn!"

"Eject cargo-arm," Morgan ordered his copilot. Once it floated free, Morgan turned the ship to go after his drifting crewmate, relying initially on visual observations provided by Saito. "Give me a bearing, Benji, where is she?"

"*Horizon.* Acknowledge abort."

Guided by Saito, Morgan managed to get within a hundred feet of Carillo by the time the doomed DoD payload began to break up from the stresses of its high-speed tumble, sending pieces flying back toward the Shuttle.

"*Horizon*, alter course immediately!"

Fearing the debris would damage the Shuttle, or further endanger the drifting Carillo, Morgan made a fateful decision. Silencing his headset, he turned control of the ship over to his copilot with a pair of terse instructions. "Change course and I'll beat your ass. Keep us as close to Carillo as possible."

While Houston continued to demand *Horizon* veer away from the path of satellite debris, Morgan headed for the cargo bay airlock, where he began to put on his spacesuit.

Mission Control, monitoring the ship's functions, noticed the activation of the display and control module on Morgan's suit. "Commander, *Horizon*. Sensors indicate EVA prep in progress. Report."

Morgan ignored their hails and clipped into an experimental jet pack stored in the airlock. It had last been used in 1985, but Morgan was familiar with it. He had been the guinea pig who tested it during a spacewalk on a previous Shuttle flight.

Before Mission Control could piece together what was happening, Morgan pulled an oxygen mask from the airlock control panel. He took several deep breaths of pure oxygen, cast aside the mask, locked his helmet into place and exited the airlock. By the time he activated the jet pack, Mission Control had surmised Morgan's plan. "Commander, *Horizon*. Abort EVA. Repeat, abort! Acknowledge!"

Morgan never considered his own safety. He knew he risked decompression sickness or death, and he knew the jet pack might fail, but there was no way he was going to watch one of his crew float away into oblivion from his seat on the flight deck.

To the amazement of his speechless crewmates aboard *Horizon*, Morgan fired the jet pack, captured his comrade and returned to the ship in the span of ten minutes. While the satellite was lost, the Shuttle escaped major damage and Morgan saved Carillo.

The rescue did come with consequences, however. Morgan incurred the bends as a result of skipping NASA's multihour airlock decompression protocol, though it only affected his joints and he recovered by the time *Horizon* returned to Earth. In addition, the flight director relieved him of command for the duration of the mission for disobeying the repeated abort orders.

Upon returning to Earth, however, a board of inquiry cleared Morgan of wrongdoing. The crew contended Mission Control's communications had been garbled and none of them had heard Houston's abort commands.

Given the classified nature of the mission, no word of the satellite mishap, Morgan's daring rescue or his disciplinary hearing ever made it into the public domain. He never went into space again but he never regretted his decision. And his courageous actions made him an instant legend among his astronaut brothers and sisters, earning him the nickname "Skywalker."

Thus, he had been the perfect choice to serve as CAPCOM for the Cetus mission. His experience, grace under pressure and heroic actions provided the crew of *Cetus Prime* a "been there, done that, have the patch to prove it" advocate and advisor at Mission Control.

These traits were especially important given the critical nature of the mission — and the inexperience of the crew. Though none of the NASA brass would admit it, they thought it unlikely the astronauts aboard *Cetus Prime* would return to Earth. As such, they chose a group of eager rookies whose thirst to explore trumped their sense of danger. NASA knew full well that balance would shift the longer the mission wore on, and when it did they wanted a level-headed compatriot for the crew to lean on. Someone who could coax them to press on when things got tough. Someone they admired and respected. Someone they would not want to fail.

Morgan understood his role and accepted the assignment primarily because he knew the green crew was being led to the wolves. But first he had tried to convince the mission director, Dennis Pritchard, to let him pilot *Cetus Prime* instead of Avery Lockett.

"Look, Dennis," Morgan had said. "These are pups we're talking about. They need someone more seasoned than Lockett."

"It's not my decision, Paul," Pritchard had replied. "DoD wants an active-duty officer at the helm. And don't sell Lockett short. He's had combat experience. He's been in high-stress situations."

"I don't care if he's freaking Captain America, he's never been in space," Morgan had countered.

Pritchard rejected the plea. Only later, when *Cetus Prime* was three months into its flight to Mars, did Morgan learn the real reason he'd been passed over for the ship's command. Over a late-night bottle of whiskey, a drunk Morgan had complained to Pritchard about the snub. An equally lit Pritchard told him, "Damn it, Paul! Don't you get it! They aren't going to make it back. Strike that. It will be a miracle if they do. NASA couldn't risk losing its biggest hero to these blasted UMOs."

As Morgan read the "beekeeper" message from Avery, he thought of that conversation with Pritchard. And of the half-truths he'd been forced to relay to the crew about the MAG-SAT experiment results. While he knew the powers that be at NASA and the Pentagon cared about the mission's success, he was increasingly concerned about their commitment to the crew. The top brass would never overtly declare the crew expendable, but Morgan sensed that sentiment growing the farther *Cetus Prime* traveled away from Earth.

It was the reason Morgan had taken to wearing a button clipped to his ID badge with the astronauts' official flight photo. He also taped candid pictures of each around the display of his CAPCOM console. The pictures had been taken at a prelaunch picnic held in the crew's honor and showed them in casual summer attire, talking and laughing with other members of the mission team. Morgan couldn't force the decision makers to keep the crew's welfare in their thoughts, but he could damn well make sure they were reminded of them.

And he could also make sure Avery and his crew weren't completely in the blind, even if he wasn't authorized to fully disclose certain developments. His decision to transmit Dr. Braun's message to Christine the previous day without editing out Braun's gravitation toward the Pentagon's predator theory was one such act. He had felt an obligation to warn the crew, and looking at Avery's reply, Morgan was relieved to know his warning had been received.

Pritchard had been livid when he found out about the unedited Braun missive, questioning Morgan's loyalty when he confronted him. Morgan could recall every word of the exchange.

"What the hell good does it do now? They're there. We can't do anything to help them," Pritchard said.

"Bull!" Morgan bellowed. "We can tell them to leave *Andromeda* in hibernation. Better yet, tell them to turn around and haul ass out of there."

"You know that's not my call. This is a joint mission. I can't abort it without buy-in from above and General Ferris."

"They're prepping to wake the probes, Dennis. Tomorrow. We can't wait any longer. If they launch *Andromeda* and the UMOs detect its X-ray generator, they're dead."

"You don't know that," Pritchard said.

"You're joking, right? You saw what the UMOs did to the XGEN-SAT…and there were only two dozen of them. What happens if *Cetus Prime* runs into a swarm with hundreds of them, like *Phobos-2* did?"

"Ferris contends the XGEN test was inconclusive. He won't support aborting the mission."

"Who gives a bleep? The crew should be told of the potential risk," Morgan said.

"Use your head, Paul, not your heart. If we tell them to deactivate the X-ray generator, there's no guarantee the UMOs still won't attack. As Ferris pointed out in the debrief, neither *Phobos-2* nor *Mars Observer* had XGENs onboard."

"Yeah, but *Phobos-2* had an X-ray spectrometer and both *Phobos-2* and *Mars Observer* had gamma-ray spectrometers," Morgan said. "The XGEN-SAT test may be telling us the UMOs are sensitive to high-frequency, high-wavelength electromagnetic radiation."

"That may be," Pritchard said, "but spectrometers don't generate X-rays or gamma rays, Paul. You know that. They only detect and collect the rays."

"True, but spectrometers do interact with the rays they collect, and they do excite them to separate waves of different intensities," Morgan said. "Who knows, maybe they create electromagnetic noise that the UMOs consider dangerous."

"I hardly think spectrometers create detectable electromagnetic interference, especially in space," Pritchard said.

"Not to us, but maybe to them. Think about how the right tone can shatter glass, or how dogs howl at sounds we can't hear. The UMOs may be very sensitive to artificially created EMI, even at levels we find undetectable," Morgan said.

"If that's the case, how do you explain the fact that there are more than a dozen X-ray telescopes orbiting Earth, each with spectrometers, and not one of them has ever been attacked?" Pritchard asked. "Face it, all we learned from the XGEN test is that the UMOs may have a potential sensitivity to the broadcast of X-rays. And, remember, we boosted the hell out of the X-ray signals in order to generate any interest from the UMOs."

"Regardless, I think we should tell them to shut down all their spectrometers until after they try to locate the debris with cameras."

"Look, without *CPO*'s spectrometers, it will be impossible for *Cetus Prime* to locate debris from *Phobos-2* and *Mars Observer*. And without *Andromeda*'s X-ray generator, they can't examine the internal damage in any debris they do find. We need to know whether the damage was random or selective. It's the whole purpose of the mission!"

"Dennis, *Andromeda* has better cameras than *Phobos-2* had," Morgan said. "Assuming pieces of *Phobos-2* and *Mars Observer* are still in orbit, and there's no guarantee of that, *Andromeda* can maneuver close enough to get the intel we need without blasting the debris with X-rays. We should tell them to turn off their XRS and GRS and try to locate the debris with other instruments."

"We're not telling them to turn the spectrometers off. End of discussion," Pritchard said.

"Okay, but we should at least tell them about what happened in the experiment," Morgan argued. "They should at least know the risk of attack if they leave the X-ray equipment on."

"Paul, no one wants to risk an attack on *Cetus Prime*, but these astronauts knew the risks, and they have a mission to fulfill, even if it costs them their lives. That's the deal they signed up for."

As Pritchard walked away, Morgan said, "Yeah, but they took the deal trusting we would have their backs. We should tell Avery. Let him make the call. That's what he's there to do."

At 1810 UTC, a routine data downlink from *Cetus Prime* was relayed to Mission Control's computer system by NA-

SA's Deep Space Network. As the downloaded data began to populate the screens at each station, Pritchard received a flurry of updates.

"Flight, CP has initiated a roll," came the voice of the guidance, navigation and control officer.

"Roger, Guidance," Pritchard said.

Then came an update from the instrumentation and communications officer. "Flight, INCO. CP reporting a pallet sep-fault. It's *Perseus*."

"EVO here, Flight," said the extravehicular activity officer. "Crew airlock being prepped for EVA."

Pritchard moved to each station to review the new data. Morgan joined him, a printout of Avery's "beekeeper" message in his hand. At 1822 UTC, the INCO officer said, "CAPCOM. Incoming alert from Commander Lockett."

With Pritchard at his side, Morgan returned to his console and opened Avery's alert.

"*CDR to CC: Be advised. CP pallet incurred sep-fault during attempt to detach Perseus for SYS-CHECK. Initial DNOG inconclusive. Authorized EVA by FE to inspect Perseus dock. Will update after INSPECT complete. CDR out.*"

"Thank God they didn't try *Andromeda* first," Morgan said. He picked up Avery's earlier message and handed it to Pritchard.

The mission director read it and crumpled the sheet of paper. As he handed the balled-up message back to Morgan, Pritchard said, "Nice going. You know Ferris is going to see this, if he hasn't already."

Morgan stood and said, "We should tell Avery. With or without Ferris' blessing, we should tell him, right now."

Pritchard glared at him. "Confirm receipt of Avery's alert. Nothing more."

CHAPTER 5

FIRST CONTACT

CETUS PRIME
FLIGHT DECK
DATE: 04.28.1995
TIME: 2011 UTC

A very watched Nick examine the clamps that secured *Perseus'* struts to its storage platform. On the small screen, it appeared as if Nick had zeroed in on the source of the problem, leading Avery to ask, "How's it going out there, Nick?"

"The clamps won't release for some reason. There's no damage I can see. No ice, either. Must be a problem with the hydraulics after all," Nick said.

"Line's probably frozen near the clamps," Avery said.

"Shouldn't be. Temp gauge showed fluid was heated," Nick said.

"Okay, I'll go take another look at the actuator and heat pump."

"Roger that."

Avery unbuckled and removed his headset. As he prepared to leave the flight deck for the pallet control center, he noticed a flash of light pass by the cockpit windows. He blinked and the flash was gone, leaving only the silhouette of Mars surrounded by the black void. Avery mumbled, "Uh-oh."

He pressed the intercom button on the center console. "Heads up, folks. Think we have visitors."

Christine, already at the pallet control center, saw the lights appear on the monitor before Avery spoke. At impossible speed, they swirled around the pallet...and Nick.

"Whoa," Nick said, as three zoomed between his legs.

Christine gripped her headset and pressed the microphone against her lips. "Hurry! Get to the airlock!"

She unbuckled from her seat and pushed off the walls to shoot toward the crew compartment airlock.

As Avery strapped back into the commander's seat, Nick said over the intercom, "Jesus, I can feel them all around me."

A loud thump echoed through the ship. Avery heard Nick let loose a string of expletives just as the ship rolled to the right. The vessel's automated reaction control system fired thrusters to compensate for the roll. The sound of creaking metal and the buzz from the UMOs could be heard throughout the ship.

Outside, the UMOs began to whip around the pallet in tight circles, causing the ship to roll in the direction of their rotation. Nick bounced against the pallet girders each time the RCS thrusters tried to steady the ship. Electrical discharges shot out from the spinning UMOs, sending thin bolts of lightning toward the probes, antennas and other instrumentation ringing the pallet. Nick closed his eyes and tried to reach for the fuselage handrail.

"Nick? Nick? Are you okay?" Christine asked, her hands shaking.

She heard him utter a growling scream and then a loud pop sounded through her headset.

"Nick, talk to me!" she said.

Throughout *Cetus Prime*'s main cabin, the electrical systems went haywire. Lights and video monitors flickered on and off. Here and there, switches overloaded, shooting out sparks and trails of smoke. Alarms pealed and red buttons flashed.

Avery switched off computer control of the RCS and manually fired thrusters, trying to shake loose from the forces compelling the ship to roll. The groan of rending metal spiked louder.

"Hold on," he called out over the intercom. "Can't hold it any longer. Either we roll or rip in two."

He deactivated the thrusters and the ship bucked to the right. *Cetus Prime* began to spin. Another loud pop and the ship went dark.

The ship tumbled for fifteen minutes before the UMOs finally halted the spin and departed, leaving *Cetus Prime* adrift without power. Batting away smoke, Avery fumbled for the flashlight in the emergency pouch attached to his seat. It was pitch dark in the cockpit and Mars was no longer visible through the cockpit windows.

Through the flight deck hatch, Avery heard Christine coughing. He leaned over and shouted toward the open hatchway, "You okay, Chris?"

"The whole ship's dead," she shouted back, her voice trembling. "What are we going to do?"

"Is there anything on fire back there?"

"No. Just smoke."

"Thank God for that," Avery whispered. He found the flashlight and turned it on. Pointing it down through the hatch, he called to Christine, "Can you see my flashlight?"

"Yes."

"Okay. Follow it. We need to restore power; I need your help."

"What if we can't? What are we going to do?"

"We'll get her restarted, I'm not worried about that," Avery said, trying his best to maintain a level tone.

Christine's ballcap appeared through the hatch as she mounted the middeck ladder. When her face rose into view, Avery redirected the flashlight to Nick's copilot seat. "Buckle in."

"Oh, my God," she said. "What about Nick? Is he dead?"

"I don't know, but we can't get him back inside until we have power, so let's get to it," he said.

She glided into the copilot's seat and tried to strap in, but her hands were shaking so bad she couldn't snap the buckles. Avery doused the flashlight and reached for her left hand. It was cold and clammy. He squeezed it and said, "Hey, hang in there, okay? We got this."

"I'm scared," she said, returning his squeeze.

"Me, too, but we have to stay focused. Okay?" Avery said. "I think the UMOs shorted out our power grid. That would've tripped circuit breakers in the engine control room. I need to go back there and reset the breakers, then we can try to power up."

Christine nodded and released Avery's hand to finish buckling into the safety harness. When done, she held her hands to her mouth and blew on them. "It's getting cold."

"Yeah, I know," Avery said. Without power, pressurization was dropping in the main cabin, and with it went their source of heat and oxygen. He removed his harness and relit the flashlight. "Be right back."

As Avery floated into the laboratory, he shined the flashlight toward the rear of the cabin. The smoke hanging in the air obscured his view, so he clicked off the torch and let his eyes adjust to the darkness. At once, he noticed a faint glow coming through the laboratory and pallet portholes, presumably coming from the sun's reflection off Mars, giving Avery a sense of their altered orientation. They'd been pushed from their intended course and spun about, away from the sun and Mars.

He passed from the laboratory into the crew compartment and was thankful to find the smoke thinning out. He listened for sounds of leaks, but the ship was silent, save for the creaking of the ship's hull. He looked to his right and spotted the crew-cabin airlock. Avery thought of Nick and wondered if he was alive and still attached to his tether, so violent had been the spinning.

Reaching the engine control room, Avery pulled open the main circuit breaker box. To his relief, all of the breakers had been tripped. As he toggled them to their "on" positions, he heard the hum of devices beginning to restart. The cabin lights also began to flicker and the ventilation system kicked in. In the distance, he heard Christine shout, "Yes!"

There were ancillary circuit breakers in each cabin that would need to be reset, but before addressing those, Avery wanted communications restored. He propelled himself back toward the flight deck and called out to Christine, "Chris, open the circuit breaker panel above the center console. Flip all the switches on. Give me a shout when you're done."

Seconds later, she shouted back, "Done."

Avery pressed the intercom button on the nearest control panel. "Nick? Nick? Can you hear me, Nick?"

There was no answer. Avery pushed off the wall and floated back to the pallet porthole. Nick was not visible. As he moved to check the airlock window, he heard Christine's voice over the intercom. "Cameras are back online. He's still out there! I can see him!"

"Where?" Avery asked.

"He's under the pallet. His tether is wrapped around *CPO*," she said.

Avery spun and propelled his body to the pallet control center. On the video monitor, he spotted the same view Christine described. Nick was bobbing against the underside of the pallet beneath *CPO*'s platform. His suit and helmet appeared intact, but given Nick's distance from the camera, it was hard to be certain. Avery checked his watch. Nick had been outside for just under an hour, meaning he had five hours of oxygen left if his tanks were undamaged.

"Okay, I see him, too," Avery said. "Check the bio-monitor. Does he have vitals?"

"Monitor's not working."

"Copy that," Avery said. "I'm going to suit up and go out and get him."

"You want help?"

"No. I need you to go through each compartment and get the rest of the circuit breakers back on," Avery said. "And see if we have comms with Goddard."

The two-hour-long wait inside the airlock was maddening, but necessary for Avery to rid his body of nitrogen and adapt to the pure oxygen he would breathe in his suit and the lower air pressure he would experience in space. During the delay, he had Christine perform diagnostic checks on the ship's core systems, asking her to relay updates after each evaluation. In addition to providing him with critical information, Avery hoped the tasks would settle her nerves.

To Avery, Christine's reports painted a hopeful picture. The ship appeared to have survived the UMO attack with minimal damage, though a more extensive damage assessment would be necessary to obtain a full picture of their situation. They had main cabin power and life support, but the ship's engines were out and they only had partial thruster control. In addition, several of their pallet instruments were inoperable, including their primary antenna for communicating with NASA.

Christine's report about the instrumentation confirmed Avery's own visual observations. Before entering the airlock, he had scrutinized the pallet on the video monitor in the control center. There, he saw the jagged remains of several instruments, damage Avery judged as more of an inconvenience than a crisis. They had backups for the most critical instrumentation and work-arounds for others.

The most immediate concern was Nick's status. He still had not responded to any of their queries and he'd shown no signs of movement. In addition, when the bio-monitoring system finally came back online, Christine had informed him that Nick's readings were all flatlined.

Avery was not surprised. However, the news didn't mean Nick was dead. It was possible the barrage of electrical discharges from the UMOs had disabled the bio-monitor electrodes in the bodysuit Nick wore underneath his spacesuit. He might just be unconscious.

Of course, it was more likely that Nick was dead, either from a direct jolt from the UMOs or from a puncture in his suit or helmet during the ship's high-speed spin. But until proven otherwise, Avery was holding out hope Nick was still alive.

Once the oxygenation and depressurization process was complete, Avery cranked open the airlock door and secured his tether to the handrail running alongside *Cetus Prime*'s fuselage, just as Nick had done. He was tempted to use his SAFER thrusters to speed his spacewalk to reach Nick but decided to preserve the emergency thruster's fuel in case the UMOs returned. As he headed for the pallet, Avery inspected the ship's hull for damage. Save for the damaged instrumentation he'd already observed, he saw none.

Arriving at the pallet, Avery pushed off the fuselage and grabbed hold of the railing along the outer girder closest to Nick. He called out again to Nick as he neared his dangling body. Still no reply. Nick's tether was wrapped tight around the feet of the *CPO* probe and there was no way Avery could untangle it while it was still attached to Nick. This meant unclipping Nick from the line and attaching him to Avery's line, making the return to the airlock an awkward venture. Avery deemed it manageable if he used the SAFER thrusters to propel them most of the way. He reached and grabbed hold of Nick's arm. "Got you, buddy."

Nick's limp arm complied with Avery's tug, but there was no other response from the stricken astronaut. As he readied to spin Nick around to examine his helmet and DCM life-support display, Avery said a quick prayer. Then, with a light pull, he spun Nick's body to face him.

Avery exhaled a sigh of relief when the helmet visor came into view. Though Nick's face was not visible through his golden solar shield, the helmet's glass was uncracked. And his suit appeared to be functioning, as indicated by the working DCM's gauges and LED lights.

Hope surged inside Avery. It was impossible to tell if Nick was still alive, but at least his suit was feeding him oxygen and heat. Avery wasted no further time. With Nick now fastened on his tether, Avery held on to him with one arm and fired the SAFER thrusters with the other.

"On my way back," Avery said.

"Roger that," Christine said. "Is he alive?"

"Don't know yet. His DCM is working. His suit and helmet are intact, but he's unresponsive."

Once in the airlock, Avery cranked the outer door closed. Sealed inside the chamber, he secured Nick to the airlock wall and then hooked receptacles on Nick's suit to outlets in the airlock that provided the suit with power and oxygen feeds from the ship. After hooking his own suit up to similar outlets, Avery examined Nick more closely. There were burn marks on his suit, but no punctures. His arms and legs were not mangled, and though his helmet was scraped up, it had no dents or cracks.

Christine looked through the airlock window and used the intercom to ask, "Is he breathing? Can you tell?"

The thickness of Nick's suit made it impossible for Avery to see signs of respiration, so he placed his gloved hand on Nick's midsection, just below the DCM pack. As soon as he felt the rise and fall of Nick's abdomen, Avery turned toward the airlock window and held up his thumb for Christine to see.

"Thank God," Christine said, resting her forehead against the airlock window.

"Ditto," Avery said. He smiled and patted Nick's shoulder. "Hang in there, my brother. You're gonna be fine."

After the two-hour airlock repressurization was completed, Christine opened the inner airlock and assisted Avery in removing Nick's suit. They examined him in the crew compartment, where they discovered burns on Nick's body that aligned with his bodysuit electrodes. They treated his burns and hooked him up to the crew quarter's medical diagnostic equipment. He was still unconscious and his vital signs were weak.

"Should we try to wake him?" Christine asked.

"Let's give it a bit to see if he comes out of it on his own," he said. "I'm hoping it's just a concussion."

"Okay," she said. "What now? Try *Perseus* again?"

"No, first we need to get the engines back online," Avery said.

"But what if the UMOs come back? Shouldn't we—"

"Listen, right now, the ship's a sitting duck. We need maneuverability more than we need anything else," Avery said.

"What good will that do? You saw how fast they were. We can't outrun them," Christine said. Avery noticed her hands trembling again.

"True, we can't. But if we have maneuverability, we can alter course, put some distance between us and Mars. Hopefully enough distance to buy us time to do a full-scale damage assessment, figure out how to communicate with Goddard and discuss next steps."

"But—"

"Christine, think. They zapped the hell out of the pallet. They might have damaged *Perseus*. We need to make sure everything checks out before we try and launch it again. We don't want it to blow up, right?"

She lowered her head and sighed. Sensing Christine was about to lose her composure, Avery said, "Hey, look at me. I need my rhino tamer to step up. Right here, right now."

Raising her head, she nodded. "I know, I know. I'll try."

"Good. While I'm getting the engines back online, I need you to go through your instruments, see if we captured any data, any video, during the attack. See what you can piece together about what happened."

CHAPTER 6

BLACKOUT

CETUS PRIME MISSION CONTROL
GODDARD SPACE FLIGHT CENTER
DATE: 04.28.1995
TIME: 2040 UTC

A t 2030 UTC, the Mission Control dayshift began to hand off to the night shift. At each station, the dayshift specialists were briefing their nightshift counterparts on the day's developments. Given Nick's impending EVA, Pritchard and Morgan opted to remain until the spacewalk was completed and the sep-fault issue resolved.

The briefings had included updates transmitted by *Cetus Prime*'s computers after Avery's alert. The EVO officer reported Nick's EVA preparation was almost complete. The emergency, environmental and consumables management officer noted Nick's vital signs during depressurization appeared nominal and his spacesuit life support was operating within parameters. The guidance officer confirmed *Cetus Prime* was still on course to insert into Mars' orbit on schedule, while the instrumentation and communications officer indicated the sep-fault error message was still active.

Amid the din of the briefings, INCO reported the first sign of trouble at 2040. "Uh, Flight?"

"Flight, here, INCO," Pritchard said. "What's up, Bobby?"

"We didn't receive CP's 2030 downlink from DSN, so I called the DSN duty officer. They say the network's not the issue. They say no downlink was transmitted."

"Hmmm, that's odd," Pritchard said. "Check CP's last downlink. Any issues with their X-band antenna?"

"I believe all comm links were green, Flight. Checking again, stand by," replied INCO. "Flight, X-band antenna was nominal at 2000."

"Copy, INCO," Pritchard said. "Send out a ping to CP, all bands. Alert DSN and TDRS to notify us as soon as they get a response."

"Copy, Flight."

Cetus Prime carried four antennas, each capable of communicating with NASA, albeit on different radio bands. The X-band antenna was the ship's highest-speed and most powerful communication link. Its signals were beamed to NASA's Deep Space Network, a collection of radio telescopes employed by NASA to track spacecraft far from Earth.

The ship's other three antennas were less powerful; hence data transmissions took more time to flow back and forth with Mission Control. At the higher end of these less-desirable communication devices was the ship's Ku-band antenna. Next on the spectrum was *Cetus Prime*'s S-band antenna, and the team's least powerful and slowest antenna was reserved for UHF-band communications. None of these lesser devices communicated with the DSN telescopes. Instead, they were picked up by a network of NASA satellites known as TDRS, or tracking and data relay satellites. The TDRS network was used primarily for near-Earth communications, but in a pinch they could be used to send and receive communications with deep space vessels.

The light chatter around the center began to subside as each station became aware of the missing downlink. When *Cetus Prime* missed another transmission at 2100, and then failed to respond to pings sent to its four antennas, silence blanketed Mission Control.

Pritchard paced the crowded room while Morgan stared at his console pictures of Avery, Christine and Nick. For eighteen minutes, time seemed to stand still.

Finally, at 2118 UTC, INCO's excited voice raced through the headsets of all in the room. "Flight, TDRS just received a return ping from CP on S-band."

Pritchard halted his pacing and began barking commands. "CAPCOM, prep CDR request for CP status. INCO, initiate system diagnostic queries via S-band uplink. EECOM, ditto on crew vitals. Guidance, get a fix on her position. Get to work, people. Let's find out what the hell's going on!"

Within the hour, data began to trickle back, and the picture was bleak. *Cetus Prime* was adrift, off course. System malfunction alarms appeared on every station screen. The crew bio-monitor was inoperable and there had been no reply from Avery or the other crew members, despite repeated requests for an update.

There were only two pieces of data that provided any glimmer of hope. EECOM reported main cabin life support was operational, and the crew compartment airlock was in the process of depressurizing.

Pritchard signaled for Morgan to follow him to a quiet corner of the room. There, Pritchard removed his headset, layering it around his neck. "Looks like they were attacked, you concur?"

"It's a strong possibility," Morgan said, "but not the only one. *Perseus* might have exploded. That would account for the dead engines and the pallet instrument failures."

"Yeah, but the main cabin would have been torn open if *Perseus* exploded," Pritchard said.

"Not necessarily. If Nick was able to resolve the sep-fault, and they deployed *Perseus*, they would have waited to fire the engine until it was clear of the ship. If the probe engine exploded, it could have knocked out *CP*'s engines and damaged the pallet without debris striking the main cabin."

"Okay, I agree. That's plausible," Pritchard said. "What do you make of the airlock depress?"

"Well, last data we had showed Nick had begun his EVA. Whether UMOs attacked or *Perseus* blew up, he'd have been in real trouble out there."

"So, you think they're attempting a rescue?"

"Or they're retrieving his body," Morgan said, his tone grim. "But we're jumping too far ahead. There could be lots of reasons for another EVA. They may be trying to assess damage, fix the X-band antenna, repair the engines. Who knows? Without comms from them, without more data, it's tough to pin down the purpose of the EVA."

"True," Pritchard said. "Why do you think they haven't responded to our hails? They must have thought to check the other bands with X-band out."

"I don't know," Morgan said, "but assuming something catastrophic happened, if I were in Avery's shoes right now, I'd be hustling to save the ship, save the crew. Talking to Mission Control would be the last thing on my mind."

"Well, we can't do anything to help them until they talk to us," Pritchard said.

"I know, but we should still keep trying to reach them," Morgan said. "Tell them we know they're in trouble. Tell them what we see in the data. Offer suggestions, encouragement. Help them realize they're not alone. And I'll tell you what else we should do: we should get off the pot and tell them about the XGEN-SAT test. Tell them to shut down their spectrometers and disable the XGEN on *Andromeda*."

"You don't give up, do you?" Pritchard said, exasperation filling his voice. "Look, they didn't launch *Andromeda*, so its XGEN was never active. And you said it yourself, an attack's not the only scenario for their situation."

"Does it freaking matter at this point, Dennis? Whatever the cause, they're hanging on by their fingernails. Unless we get a miracle, the mission is screwed. We should be focused on saving our people," Morgan said, tapping the photo button pinned to his badge.

CETUS PRIME
LABORATORY COMPARTMENT
DATE: 04.28.1995
TIME: 2310 UTC

Avery was able to restart the engines without incident, allowing him to calculate and guide *Cetus Prime* into a wider elliptic around Mars. With the maneuver completed, he checked in on Nick again. He was still unconscious, but his vital signs had improved. Avery then returned to the lab for a progress update on Christine's analysis.

"I've been able to extract data from some of the instruments, but nothing's jumped out so far. I'll keep looking," she said.

"Okay, sounds good," Avery said. "By the way, I checked the comms system. X-band antenna is out, same with Ku. But the S-band and UHF antennas are working. Goddard's using S-band; they're aware of our situation. I sent them a quick update. Once I'm done with the damage assessment, let's get back together and compare notes. Then we'll send them a full report, see what they want us to do."

CETUS PRIME MISSION CONTROL
GODDARD SPACE FLIGHT CENTER
DATE: 04.28.1995
TIME: 2330 UTC

The nightshift INCO leapt from his seat. "Flight! We have a new message from Commander Lockett!"

Applause and cheers erupted in Mission Control. Pritchard instructed the officer to read out the message.

"Copy that." INCO read aloud: "CDR to GSC: CP attacked by UMOs during FE EVA to repair *Perseus* sepfault. FE unconscious, vitals stable. Request medical treatment guidance. CDR and MS unharmed. Cursory DA shows minimal damage, mostly pallet instrumentation.

Full DA underway. Have altered course to assume wider Mars orbit. Coordinates to follow. COMMS spotty, S-band and UHF only. Hands full, but working the problems. Will provide sit-rep when full DA complete. CDR out."

A collective sigh of relief spread through the room. Within minutes, INCO announced the arrival of *Cetus Prime*'s 2340 systems diagnostics report, commenting, "Commander Lockett must have reset the system."

The station leaders, and their dayshift counterparts, began to analyze the new data. Morgan darted a look at Pritchard, who was engaged in a conversation with the flight surgeon. Turning back to his console, Morgan gazed at the crew's pictures and then began typing. When finished, he hovered his finger over the send button and reviewed the message.

"*CC to CDR: Message received. Standing by to assist. Medical guidance to follow. Disable XGEN on Andromeda until further notice. Same with XRS and GRS on all vehicles. Repeat: DISABLE ALL XRAY AND GAMMA EQUIP ASAP. CC Out.*"

After looking back once more at Pritchard, Morgan pressed the button and said, "Screw it."

A single line appeared on the monitor: "Message sent."

CHAPTER 7

BARKS AND BITES

CETUS PRIME
LABORATORY COMPARTMENT
DATE: 04.29.1995
TIME: 0042 UTC

n the middle of Avery's damage assessment, Christine called him to the lab. As soon as he floated into the compartment, she blurted, "I don't think it was an attack."

"What?" Avery queried.

"I think it was more of a reconnaissance, a scouting party," she said. She directed his attention to a video monitor showing the lights moving around the pallet. "See. They didn't swarm. And it looks like there were only a dozen of them."

"Twelve? Twelve of them were capable of spinning the ship?" he asked.

"That's right," she said. "Scary."

"Hell, yeah."

"As you can see, they acted independently until they started to spin the pallet, but even then, they didn't swarm. They grouped together in a formation, but they didn't swarm."

"Hmmm."

"I think I know what attracted them, too," she said. Christine pointed to the X-ray spectrometer. "Watch."

Avery looked at the screen. The XRS showed a wavy line with narrow peaks and valleys.

"All our spectrometers were active, looking for signs of radiation on our Mars approach. I was hoping we might pick up a blip from *Phobos-2* or *Mars Observer* debris before we deploy *CPO*. What you see here is pretty normal stuff. Background radiation," she said. "Then, right before the UMOs showed up…"

The wavy line went berserk. Huge spikes filled the screen.

"The readings went on like this until the power went out," she said. "All of our other instrumentation maintained nominal readings until the UMOs started zapping the pallet."

"And one of the things they zapped was the pallet XRS. They took out the GRS as well," Avery said. "I saw what's left of them from the porthole."

"Right. So, I know this sounds a little out there, but here's a theory. All animals have some form of sensory threat detection. Visual. Auditory. Olfactory. Even changes in the Earth's magnetic field can signal threats to certain animals who have receptors capable of detecting the changes.

"Now, we know our UMOs are electromagnetic lifeforms, and we know they feed on ions. But we don't necessarily know what kinds of ions they prefer to consume and which ones they consider dangerous."

"You think they considered our X-ray spectrometer a threat?" Avery asked.

"I think it's possible. Remember, Mars' atmo is very thin. Not a lot of ions to be had there. If there's a 'hive' of these things living around Mars or Phobos, their food supply is pretty scarce. Anything that disrupts or endangers that food supply would be considered an imminent threat," Christine said.

"But the XRS just collects X-rays. Why would they consider it a threat?" Avery asked.

"I don't know, but back on Earth, they've been hanging out between our magnetosphere and ionosphere. Not a lot of X-rays there. Mostly VLF waves."

"So..."

"Well, VLF waves are very low frequency forms of electromagnetic radiation, hence the name. X-rays, on the other hand, are at the opposite end of the spectrum. Very high frequency radiation," Christine said.

"Got it. So, they're into eating VLF ions, not so much X-ray ions."

"Either that or maybe X-rays are like a blight to their food source," Christine said. "What's weird is they are capable of emitting X-rays. That's what I think generated the spikes. They sensed our spectrometer, then emitted X-rays to locate the ship, broadcasting them like sonar. There's no other explanation I can think of to account for the spike in readings. A passing comet might emit X-rays on that kind of scale, but not that sudden."

"Hmmm…Still doesn't answer why our spectrometer would attract them," Avery said.

"As I said, I don't have an answer for that. But, if you recall, *Phobos-1* and 2 had X-ray spectrometers. *Mars Observer* didn't, but it did have a gamma-ray spectrometer."

"But our GRS didn't spike?" Avery asked.

"Not until they started shooting lightning bolts," she said.

"Why didn't they swarm and destroy us, I wonder," Avery said.

"Proximity to their food source?" Christine ventured. "*Phobos-2* and *Mars Observer* were a lot closer to Mars when they were attacked."

"Makes sense," Avery said. "Two curve balls for you. They also took out the X-band antenna. It's not a huge problem; we can use the S-band antenna in the short term, and we have a backup X-band in the storage bay we can hook up later. But why did they zap that, too? It's on the other side of the pallet, and it doesn't emit X-rays or gamma rays."

"Could be something to do with the concentration of the radio beam. X-band sends very condensed signals, even though X-band waves are much lower frequency compared to X-rays. Maybe the UMOs are also sensitive to boosted signals. I'll have to give it some more thought."

"Okay, while you're doing that, here's another riddle. Why the spin? Why disable our power? They were obviously able to zero in on the spectrometers, take them out. Same with the antenna. So, what was their purpose in spinning the ship? Knocking out our power? Zapping some of the other instruments?"

"I've been wondering that myself," she said. "From a biology perspective, the spinning behavior may have been their way of issuing a warning. Lots of animals use physical gestures to ward off predators, competitors. Spread their wings, whip their tails, circle the threat, bark, those kinds of things. Maybe the spin was the UMOs' way of barking."

"All right," Avery said. "I can buy that. So, they detected the spectrometer and came to check us out to see if we were the ones generating the threat. They determined we were the source and spun the ship to warn us to knock off with the spectrometer. We didn't respond, so they zapped the instruments. In the process, they hit us hard enough to knock out our power, but not hard enough to destroy the ship."

"It fits, don't you think?" Christine said. "It's common for animals to bite or sting a threat encroaching on their territory to send a message without killing the source of the threat. It's their way of telling the threat to back off."

"Right. So, we should ixnay the X-rays," Avery said. "Which means we need to disable the XGEN on *Andromeda* and our XRSs. Probably should do the same with gammas."

"Goddard won't like it," Christine said. "We're supposed to use the spectrometers on *CPO* to help find *Phobos-2* and

Mars Observer, and *Andromeda*'s XGEN to examine the debris. But I'm with you. It's not worth risking another attack."

"Agreed. You disable the software. I'll send a message to Goddard, tell them why we're doing it. Let's just hope they see it our way," Avery said. As he prepared to leave, he paused and turned to Christine. "Hey."

"Yeah?"

"Good to see *Tamasha ya Rhino* back in action!"

CHAPTER 8

TAKE THE HILL

MISSION CONTROL BRIEFING ROOM
GODDARD SPACE FLIGHT CENTER
DATE: 04.29.1995
TIME: 0114 UTC

P ritchard watched Ferris' face turn purple as he read the string of messages between Morgan and Avery. The general had been at the Pentagon when Goddard first learned of *Cetus Prime*'s run-in with the UMOs. Since then, the Air Force duty officer at the DoD station in Mission Control had provided his superior with updates as they occurred. One of the updates had been Morgan's last message to Avery. Messages between CAPCOM and *Cetus Prime* were copied to Pritchard and the DoD officer, given the joint nature of the mission.

Ferris hadn't wasted time calling to chew out Pritchard. He hopped in the back of a blacked-out SUV and arrived at Goddard within a half hour. When he arrived, the Air Force duty officer handed him a stack of the last two days' worth of back-and-forth communiques. Ferris appeared long enough in the Mission Control Center to summon Pritchard to join him in the briefing room.

Of all the messages, the last two were on the page Ferris still held in his shaking hands. Pritchard looked down at his own copy, reading the first of Avery's most recent messages.

"*CDR to CC: All X-ray and gamma-ray EQUIP disabled. Early read of UMO attack suggests action triggered by XRS. Full analysis of UMO action and DA to follow. CDR out.*"

The message had obviously been sent before Avery read Morgan's command to shut off the equipment. Avery's final message read: "*CDR to CC: Received CC directive to disable all X-ray and gamma-ray EQUIP. Per earlier CDR message, EQUIP already disabled. DA and UMO action report still to follow. CDR out.*"

"Where is the son of a bitch?" Ferris asked.

"I relieved him of duty as soon as I saw his message to Avery. I told him to wait for me in his office," Pritchard said.

"What was he thinking?"

"You know him as well as I do, General. He's always been one of those guys who acts on instincts," Pritchard said with a shrug. "But it looks like he was right, again."

"I don't give a crap," Ferris said, pounding the table. "He broke the chain of command, violated a direct order."

"And he's been relieved because of it," Pritchard said, "but, in his defense, he was just thinking of the crew. It's his job, you know."

"The crew?" Ferris scowled. "The crew's job is to see the hill and take it, Pritchard. Now that they've seen it, it's time for them to take it."

"What's that supposed to mean?"

"It means it's time to drop the migration crap. These things are lethal killing machines. We shouldn't waste another second trying to find old debris. We ought to lure the little bastards out and see if we can kill them with the EMPs."

"And how do you propose we do that?" Pritchard asked.

"Send *Andromeda* in. Turn its XGEN on and wait for them to attack. Then blast the hell out of them with *Perseus*. Send in *Cetus Prime* afterward to see if the EMPs did the job."

"With all due respect, General, the EMPs are untested, unproven. They may have no effect on the UMOs," Pritchard said.

"Exactly. It's time to find out if they work," Ferris said.

"And what about *Cetus Prime*? The crew? What happens to them if the EMPs don't work?" Pritchard asked.

With a wave of his hand, Ferris scoffed. "Tell them to keep their spectrometers off. The UMOs will go after *Perseus*, not *Cetus Prime*."

"You don't know that," Pritchard said, rising from his chair. "I'm sorry, General. It's too risky. I'm not advocating a change of mission."

"Pritchard, I don't give a flying fuck what you think," Ferris said, reclining in his chair. "Besides, I've already teed it up with the Joint Chiefs and SECDEF. They're discussing it with the White House now."

"You've done what?"

"You heard me."

"Now, hold on a minute."

"It's too late, Pritchard. Ball's in motion."

"Not if I can do anything about it," Pritchard said, heading for the door.

"Be my guest," Ferris said.

Pritchard's phone call with NASA's chief administrator, Dr. Karen Wells, was as short as it was frustrating. Wells had already capitulated. The political appointee explained the secretary of defense had convinced the president of the change in mission before she was even consulted.

When Pritchard pressed her to go back to the White House, she demurred. "It's a done deal, Dennis. There's nothing I can do."

She explained that SECDEF had presented an ironclad case. If they risked sending the crew into Mars' orbit without the spectrometers, the chance of them finding and collecting the older probes' debris was close to zero. If they went in with the spectrometers on, there was a high probability the UMOs would attack again, this time taking out *Cetus Prime*, likely before they collected any intelligence of value. If the crew was told to turn the ship around and come home, the mission would go down as a colossal waste of time and resources and the UMOs would still pose a grave threat to national security and future space exploration.

The capper to the secretary's argument? The EMPs could not be tested in Earth's orbit. Doing so would violate nuclear treaties with Russia, and depending on which side of the bed their leadership woke up on, might incite a nuclear attack. At a minimum, it would create an international incident that would be hard for the White House to quell.

To the contrary, *Cetus Prime* was about to enter Mars' orbit. Given the earlier attack on the ship, UMOs were obviously in the vicinity. Further, the crew had the means to stimulate a swarm, now that there were two data points demonstrating the UMOs' sensitivity to X-rays. And *Cetus Prime* had the best weapon available — the only weapon available — to defeat the UMOs aboard *Perseus*. If there was ever to be an opportunity to test the EMPs, it was now.

When Wells finished relaying SECDEF's sales pitch, Pritchard asked, "But what if it goes wrong?"

"Meaning what?"

"What if the EMPs don't work?"

"Then the Pentagon will know they need to come up with a different weapon," she said.

"I'm not talking about the damn weapon. I'm talking about the crew!" Pritchard said.

Pritchard found Paul Morgan sitting in his office, staring at his picture-button of the *Cetus Prime* crew. Pritchard closed the office door, plopped down in a guest chair and uttered a deep sigh. Morgan kept his eyes on the photo and asked, "Am I fired?"

"What?"

"Have you come to fire me?"

Pritchard shook his head. "No. The opposite. I've come to apologize. You were right, and you won't believe what Ferris has done."

The mission director ran through his discussions with Ferris and Wells. When he finished, he said, "I have a very, very bad feeling about this, Paul, and I don't think we can stop it from happening."

"Probably not," Morgan said. "But we can try."

"Huh?"

Morgan rose from his chair and said, "Come with me. I've got an idea."

The two men walked through the corridors of Goddard Space Flight Center until they reached the office of the TDRS project manager, Hector Jimenez. Behind closed doors, Morgan and Pritchard filled him in on the situation.

In the middle of the conversation, Pritchard received a page from Mission Control. He stepped out of the room to call the center and returned a few minutes later. "Gotta go. Ferris is trying to pressure the CAPCOM on duty to send the new mission plan. Jesus, I hope your plan works, Paul."

"Me, too," Morgan said.

After Pritchard left, Morgan turned to Hector and asked, "So, will you do it?"

"For anyone else, hell, no," Hector said. "But for you? No one says no to Skywalker."

CHAPTER 9

BAITING THE BEAST

CETUS PRIME
CREW GALLEY
DATE: 04.29.1995
TIME: 0613 UTC

very found Christine in the crew galley picking at the last remnants of a protein bar. He had contemplated waiting until after they'd slept to tell her of Goddard's new directive, but then Morgan's secret message had arrived, necessitating an immediate conversation.

"Hi there," he said, floating into a seat next to Christine.

Without looking up, she said, "Hey."

He noticed tears on her face and a balled-up tissue tucked into the collar of her shirt. So much for the reemergence of the rhino tamer.

"You okay?" he asked.

"No," she said, her lips quivering. A teardrop floated off her cheek. "Flight surgeon had me examine Nick, run an EEG on him. He's not in a coma, he's brain dead."

Avery bowed his head and sighed. After a moment of silence, he whispered, "Damn."

"Surgeon said to take him off oxygen, suit him up and send him out the airlock," she said, her face turning beet red. She reached for the tissue and swiped it beneath her nose.

Though the treatment sounded cruel, it was the established protocol for disposing of a dead astronaut on a deep space mission. Avery asked, "Was the surgeon one hundred percent positive about Nick?"

She nodded. "Pupils unresponsive to light. No reaction to pain. No blink reflex. Flat EEG. His autonomous functions are still working, but his mind is gone."

"Damn," Avery repeated.

"I can't do it," she said, looking toward the crew quarter's compartment where Nick lay strapped to a table. "Effing NASA! Effing UMOs."

Under the circumstances, Avery was certain Christine would react poorly to the new directive from Goddard, but delaying the discussion now was not an option.

"I need to talk to you about something," he said. "And you're not going to like it."

He didn't sugarcoat his one-sentence description of the change in mission. As expected, Christine was furious. "They want us to do what? Are they effing insane?"

"They're scared," he said.

"They're scared? Join the effing party!" she growled. "Jesus, why is the solution to every problem shooting missiles at something?"

As an Air Force pilot, Avery had done his fair share of missile shooting, and on a few of those occasions, he had wondered the same thing — and in this case, he was fully planted on Christine's side.

The suggestion that they lure the UMOs with *Andromeda*'s XGEN and then shoot one of *Perseus'* EMPs at whatever showed up seemed as advisable as walking into a lion's cage slathered in fresh animal blood and baiting the beast to attack.

"Before you go nuclear," Avery said, "Paul Morgan contacted me. Unofficially. Seems he's been relieved of CAP-COM duty."

"What?"

"Yeah. Apparently, he caught crap for telling us to shut down the spectrometers. He wasn't authorized to do it."

"I don't understand. Why?"

"Braun didn't change her mind because the MAG-SAT tests failed. One of them succeeded. The UMOs destroyed a satellite broadcasting X-rays. Granted, they had to jack up the intensity of the X-rays to get them to attack," Avery said.

"What? Why didn't Braun say so?" Christine asked.

"There was a debate about the test results. A decision was made to withhold the info from us until the debate was resolved," Avery said.

Christine rubbed her temples as she processed Avery's explanation. He knew it was only a matter of seconds before she realized Goddard knew about the MAG-SAT test before the UMOs attacked *Cetus Prime* and that the attack might have been prevented had they shared the news.

"Look, it sounds harsh, but what's done is done. We can't undo what's happened, but we can change how things roll from here," Avery said. "Morgan suggested we use the *Perseus* sep-fault to stall while he tries to talk them out of their plan. But we don't have much time. Goddard wants us to launch *Andromeda* by 1300 UTC."

Christine glanced at her watch. "You're kidding me. After everything that's happened? Why the rush?"

"They don't want to risk losing contact with the UMOs that attacked us."

"What exactly is Goddard's plan?" she asked.

Avery laid it out. They were to send *Andromeda* into Mars' orbit and then turn its XGEN on. Presuming the X-rays would attract the UMOs, the crew was to fire one of *Perseus'* missiles at the swarm enveloping *Andromeda*. After the EMP exploded, the crew was to deploy *CPO* to survey the area for signs of UMOs, utilizing its high-frequency radiation spectrometers to effectively lure them out again. If none appeared, they would know the EMP worked. If *CPO* was swarmed, then either the EMP had failed or *Perseus'* missile had missed its target, and they were instructed to fire a missile at *CPO*.

"And then what?" Christine asked.

"Good question," Avery said. "We're supposed to report back our findings and wait for further instructions."

"If we're still alive, you mean," she said.

Avery thought of the time he had been playing Frisbee with his father in their backyard. Avery's errant toss had disappeared into some bushes. His father reached in to retrieve it, only to bolt away from the bush, screaming,

"Bees!" Not only did the bees go after his father, they also went after Avery and a neighbor watering her lawn on the other side of the bushes.

"I hear you," Avery said. "Morgan's of the same mindset, too. If the first EMP doesn't work, he thinks the UMOs will go after any and every electromagnetic signature in proximity to the explosion. There won't be a chance to deploy *CPO* and try again."

Christine stared off toward the laboratory compartment while Avery continued to speak. "I was thinking we might be able to create a diversion to give us time to escape."

There was no response from Christine. She seemed zoned out. Avery waved to get her attention. "Hey, Chris. Over here."

"They attacked an XGEN," she mumbled.

"Um, yeah."

"None of the other probes had XGENs," she said.

"I know," he said. "Look, can we get back to the diversion?"

She turned to face Avery and grabbed his arm. "Oh, my God. I think I know why. I think I know why they're attacking."

Before Avery could interject, Christine unbuckled and shot toward the lab. At the hatchway, she turned back and encouraged Avery to follow. While she floated to her instrument station, she began talking. "Before the flight surgeon's message came in, I was watching the video of the UMO attack again. This time in slo-mo. Their behavior was more deliberate than I'd noticed at full speed."

She held onto the countertop with one hand to keep from floating away, while tapping on a keyboard with the other. Avery came up beside her as the video screen flickered on. A few keystrokes later, the video of the pallet during the UMO attack began to play in slow motion. "See how they bumped up against the instruments, almost nuzzling against them?"

"I see what you mean," Avery said, watching the lights. "They look like moths bouncing off a bug zapper."

"A good analogy," she said, typing away on the keyboard. "Remember how I said I thought the X-ray spectrometer posed a threat to their food source?"

"Yeah."

"I think I was wrong, but we'll know for sure in a few secs. I just need to true up the video and the spectrometer readings." With the task accomplished, she replayed both feeds in slow motion, darting her eyes from one screen to the other. Avery did the same. On the X-ray spectrometer display screen, the strong spikes dissipated once the UMOs appeared on the pallet. Instead, the wave band narrowed into pulse-type spikes.

"Gah! I should have noticed that," she said, slapping the countertop. "I was too focused on the spinning behavior."

"Should have noticed what?" Avery asked.

"The UMO attacks have nothing to do with food! And Dr. Braun was right!" Christine said, glancing down at her watch. "I need to send a message to her. Right now."

"Whoa," Avery said, catching hold of Christine's leg as she began to propel herself to the communications center below the flight deck. "Slow down. Talk to me. I don't understand what you're saying."

As she floated backward, Avery caught Christine's shoulder. She turned to reveal a smile on her face. "The XGEN-SAT test. It confirms it. This is about territory, not food. My God, they behave just like honey bees."

"Explain," Avery said. "Still not getting it."

"The UMOs around Mars don't have a queen! Or she's old, beyond the age where she can replenish the colony. Either way, they're looking for a new queen. They thought the radiation emanating from the XRS was a queen sending out a signal to them. There must be something in the pulse action of the spectrometer that gives off a pheromone-like radiation," Christine said. She paused the video and XRS files and looped them back to watch again. "When bees lose a queen, they swarm and go looking for a new one. When they pick up the scent of a new queen, they surround her and together they go looking for a place to create a new hive."

"You can tell that from the video?"

"The video and readings together. When honey bees are introduced to a new queen, they surround her, rub up against her, sort of dance with her."

"Okay, with you now. So, they attacked because the queen didn't respond? Didn't dance back?"

"Exactly! Bees get royally pissed if they discover an impostor. For example, if a foreign queen enters a hive where there's already a queen in residence, the bees in the hive will attack the new one. Viciously."

"So, once the UMOs realized their mistake, they got angry," Avery said.

"Yep."

"Okay, so how does the XGEN fit in?"

"All right, remember what happened before the UMOs came toward us. They sent out strong X-ray pulses. Remember the big spikes."

"I remember. You said you thought they were using the X-rays as sonar."

"Right. That's exactly it. Only they weren't trying to locate a threat. They were telling the queen, or what they thought was a queen, 'we're here, we're coming for you.'"

"Oh, I see," Avery said. The UMOs orbiting Earth interpreted the blast of X-rays from the XGEN as a scouting party or swarm from a new colony. "The Earth UMOs thought a new colony was invading their territory, looking to take their queen."

"Exactly. Bees are very territorial. Very protective of their queen," Christine said. "I need to share this with Dr. Braun. See if she concurs. If she does, there's no reason to go through with Goddard's new plan."

She pushed off the wall and glided through the hatch into the communications center. Avery followed her and said, "It's almost three in the morning on the East Coast. She's not going to be awake."

"Probably not, but Goddard can wake her up. Besides, on the S-band, it's going to take a while to send the video and spectrometer files."

"Look, don't get your hopes up," Avery said. "You may be right, but Goddard may not agree. Space Command is pushing the buttons now. They're probably still going to want to go through with their plan. If for no other reason than to confirm your theory."

"Maybe," she said, typing her message to Dr. Braun. "But I think my theory negates the need for the plan. How often is anyone going to broadcast X-rays from a satellite in Earth orbit? Plus, you said earlier they had to really boost the signal to stimulate the attack. And their XRS tests failed to produce any effect. I think that's telling us the UMOs around Earth have their queen, and so long as nothing happens to her, they're not going to attack."

CHAPTER 10

FOR THE GREATER GOOD

CETUS PRIME MISSION CONTROL
GODDARD SPACE FLIGHT CENTER
DATE: 04.29.1995
TIME: 1213 UTC

eneral Ferris entered Mission Control. In Dennis Pritchard's headset, one of the team said, "Fire-breathing dragon at your six."

Pritchard turned to see the red-faced leader of Space Command heading right toward him. He stopped in his tracks when he saw Paul Morgan sitting at the CAPCOM station.

"What in Sam Hill is going on?" he seethed.

"Good morning, General," Pritchard said, rising from his seat.

"Stow it," Ferris said. "What's Morgan doing here? He's relieved."

"I reinstated him," Pritchard said.

"What the hell for?" Ferris asked. "He went behind your back, Pritchard. Countermanded your order."

"It was a misunderstanding. It's been sorted out," Pritchard said.

"Why isn't *Perseus* out of dock? What's all this about a delay?" Ferris demanded to know.

"The crew's provided some new information. We told them to catch some sleep while we analyze their data," Morgan said, joining the impromptu briefing.

"Jesus, Mary and Joseph," Ferris said, his voice carrying throughout the room. "Wake their asses up! Get them moving on *Perseus*."

"If their data pans out, there may not be a need to deploy *Perseus*," Morgan said.

With fists clenched at his side, Ferris said, "Get that God damn bird off the deck, do you hear me? I don't give a crap what kind of data they have, we're testing those EMPs."

"*Perseus* is staying in dock until the analysis is complete," Pritchard said. "If you want to run it up the chain, be my guest."

For a moment it appeared Ferris might start swinging, but instead he made an abrupt turn and walked away. Pritchard and Morgan watched him head for the DoD duty officer, two stations away from Pritchard's. He barked out the man's name and the two disappeared from the center.

"Think he'll go back to SECDEF? Get the president involved again?" Morgan asked.

"Probably, but at least it will buy us some more time," Pritchard said.

At 1242 UTC, Ferris reappeared in Mission Control with the duty officer. The junior officer returned to his station, while Ferris approached Pritchard. In a calm tone, he said, "Would you and CAPCOM please join me in the briefing room. I'd like to hear about this new information."

With the three men behind closed doors, Morgan provided a summary of Christine's theory, touching upon the video evidence and the XRS readings. Ferris peppered both men with a stream of questions, stopping on several occasions to take notes.

In Mission Control, the DoD duty officer layered on a headset and began typing, every so often looking around at the others in the room. Ten minutes later, he pressed one last button, powered down his station and left the room.

At 1310 UTC, with Pritchard and Morgan still huddled with Ferris, INCO received an alert from *Cetus Prime*. "Holy crap."

He bolted up out of his seat and looked toward Pritchard's station. Seeing the post vacated, he pushed the microphone of his headset toward his lips. "Flight? Flight? Anyone seen Flight?"

The EECOM officer in the row of stations in front of INCO replied, "Think Flight is in Debrief-1. Why?"

"*Andromeda* just separated from the pallet. Someone go get Flight, ASAP!"

Morgan and Pritchard burst into Mission Control and ran to their stations. INCO waved to Pritchard, pointing at his headset. Pritchard pulled his on and heard INCO say, "I can't stop it, Flight. I'm locked out. *CPO* is free, too."

"Flight, Guidance here. *CP* is turning toward Mars."

"INCO here again, Flight. S-band is out. I have no comms with *CP*."

Morgan threw down his headset. "Ferris!"

He raced out of Mission Control and back to the debriefing room, where he found the general sitting back, hands behind his head and smile on his face.

"What have you done?" Morgan yelled.

"You didn't have the balls to do what's necessary. I did," Ferris said.

Back in Mission Control, INCO's voice echoed through the headsets of everyone in the room. "Jesus, no! Flight, *Perseus* is powering up. Turret is turning!"

Pritchard tossed off his headset and made for the debrief room, too. When he came through the door, Morgan and Ferris were screaming at each other. Pritchard grabbed hold of Morgan's arm. "*Perseus* is getting ready to fire!"

"What?" Morgan said, staggering backward.

"We can't stop it, he's locked us out of all controls," Pritchard said.

Morgan took a swing at Ferris, clipping him on the chin. "Bastard."

The blow toppled the general over a chair. Morgan said to Pritchard, "Do what you can."

He pulled the conference room door open so hard the knob punched a hole in the wall. Morgan dashed down the hallway, around a corridor and up two flights of stairs. Out of breath, he burst into Hector Jimenez's office and said, "Hook me into TDRS! Now!"

CETUS PRIME
CREW QUARTERS
DATE: 04.29.1995
TIME: 1300 UTC

A captain knows his ship, even when he's asleep. The spit of the thrusters, the creak of the hull, the rumble of the engines. All the ship's sounds and motions seep into the subconscious and unconscious of a flight leader. And so, when the first thruster pushed *Cetus Prime* inward toward Mars, Avery awoke.

Then came the throaty churn of the main engines, pushing the craft forward. The sudden movement tugged at the cocoon-like bag in which Avery slept, rocking the bag back and forth. Confused, he shook his head and listened. Was it a dream? Clanks echoed from the rear of the main cabin. The high-pitched hiss of more thrusters filled the room.

This was no dream. Avery pushed out of the bag, calling to Christine. "Wake up! Something's wrong."

He didn't wait for her to answer. He propelled toward the flight deck, passing through the lab and comms center. By the time he had strapped into the commander's seat, he could see *Andromeda* and *CPO* jetting toward Mars.

He tried to override the RCS thrusters to no avail. *Cetus Prime* continued toward Mars, picking up speed. Christine appeared through the floor hatch. "What's going on?"

"Goddard's taken control of the ship! They've launched *Andromeda* and *CPO*. Get to pallet control. See if you can recall them."

Mouth open, stunned, Christine hovered in the hatchway.

"Damn it, Chris! Move your ass!"

His shout stirred Christine to action. As she disappeared through the hatch, Avery thought, "We're screwed without Nick."

Christine bounced her way to pallet control. She tried every switch, button and command she could remember. Out of the corner of her eye, she saw the turret of *Perseus* begin to turn. She gasped. "No!"

Punching the intercom button, she yelled, "*Perseus*! System's hot, she's getting ready to fire!"

In the cockpit, Avery's fingers moved with frantic precision, working through every protocol he'd been taught about the ship. Nothing worked. *Cetus Prime* lurched forward, its engines at full power. He rained down blow after blow on the console in front of him, screeching obscenities at the top of his lungs. Out of breath and out of options, he pitched back in the seat, his eyes looking upward at the array of buttons and switches above his head.

And then he saw it. The circuit breaker box. Crushing a closed fist on the intercom, he yelled to Christine, "Circuit breakers. Switch 'em off. All of them. Do it, now!"

As he spoke, he disabled the breakers in the cockpit and then descended to the comms deck. Within a minute, the breakers in every cabin were off. *Cetus Prime* was dead… but still flying toward Mars at thousands of miles per hour.

Christine met Avery in the comms center. Together, they ascended to the flight deck. As they strapped in, Christine stuttered, "Wha-what's…happ-happening?"

"We're being sacrificed for the greater good," Avery said.

Out the cockpit window, they saw a swarm of UMOs appear from the dark side of Mars, heading for *Andromeda.*

CHAPTER 11

ABANDONED

*A*ndromeda and *CPO* went up like fireworks on Independence Day. Avery and Christine watched in terror as the swarm turned toward *Cetus Prime*. Though the ship had no power, its engines still glowed hot with radiation. To Avery's chagrin, his decision to cut *Cetus Prime*'s power rendered *Perseus* impotent, leaving them no means of defense as thousands upon thousands of bright lights zoomed toward the crippled spacecraft.

CETUS PRIME MISSION CONTROL
GODDARD SPACE FLIGHT CENTER
DATE: 04.29.1995
TIME: 1410 UTC

Chaos reigned in Mission Control. Station leads, desperate to revive control over the spacecraft they'd tended for seven months, punched in abort commands, tried to reset systems, typed in override commands. Not one of them stopped working the problems...until their screens went blank at 1410 UTC.

In a remarkable demonstration of devotion, the station leads stayed on until sunset the following day, trying every trick in the book, and then some, to restore communication with their lost charge. Tears were shed, anger vented, prayers offered, but no amount of brainpower or emotion could bring them back.

Paul Morgan's last message to the crew on their UHF channel never made it through, scattering into the void of space long before it reached *Cetus Prime*'s last known position. It read, *"CC to CDR: All bets off, save yourselves! Get the hell out of there! CC out."*

EPILOGUE

When the president learned what Ferris had done, he relieved the general of command and eventually Ferris was court-martialed. A joint tribunal of NASA and DoD executives conducted an exhaustive review of the entire *Cetus Prime* mission, including a painstaking evaluation of Mission Specialist Christine Baker's "queen bee" theory.

The tribunal featured a rigorous scientific review of the data transmitted by *Cetus Prime* before communication was lost, the XGEN MAG-SAT test, and data from the earlier Phobos and *Mars Observer* missions. It also included testimony from Dr. Braun and other animal behaviorist researchers.

The conclusion: Christine Baker had been right. The UMOs were not predatory by nature. They were reacting to electromagnetic stimuli in the same way a honey bee might, confronting analogous conditions.

Astrophysicists at JPL determined the faux "queen bee" call was linked to the type of X-ray spectrometers aboard *Phobos-1* and *Phobos-2*. The Soviet RF-15 XRS produced a distinct radiation signature unlike any other model X-ray spectrometer deployed in space. As to *Mars Observer*, though it carried no XRS, its GRS produced a strikingly similar radiation signature as the RF-15.

In the twenty-three years since communication was severed with *Cetus Prime*, no American spacecraft sent to *orbit* Mars has carried an X-ray spectrometer, nor a GRS of the same model as deployed on *Mars Observer*. In that time, four other Mars probes — two American, one Japanese and one British — have mysteriously disappeared in orbit around the planet. The Japanese and British spacecraft both carried X-ray spectrometers. It is not known whether they deployed before their sudden and unexplained "lost communications."

Since the 1995 XGEN MAG-SAT test, there has never been an observed hostile act by UMOs orbiting Earth. They continue to multiply in direct proportion to the propagation of ions in the upper reaches of the planet's atmosphere and are routinely captured on video by cameras aboard the International Space Station.

Though the Mission Control Center for *Cetus Prime* was repurposed two months after losing communication with the ship, a Goddard Space Flight Center team was tasked with monitoring all four of the ship's radio bands for a period of time thereafter.

On July 18, 1995, at 2207 UTC, a corrupted data file was received by TDRS on the UHF channel. It took weeks, but a trio of radio experts plucked from NASA's DSN team were able to restore a portion of the file. It was an eight-second grainy video showing Avery Lockett and Christine Baker seated in the laboratory compartment of *Cetus Prime*. In it, Christine spoke to the camera. There was a smile on her face. On both their faces. Her words cut in and out, no matter how much the DSN radio engineers tried to resample the audio. "*...VLF antenna...don't know...taking us...*"

The date stamp of the video, displayed in the upper right-hand corner of the screen, read 06.10.1995, 0825 UTC, forty-two days after *Cetus Prime* disappeared.

NASA remains at a loss to explain the additional thirty-eight day gap between the receipt of the message by TDRS and the date stamp recorded on the video. While some suggested *Cetus Prime*'s recording system had displayed the incorrect date, others suggested the disparity indicated the crew had run into difficulties restoring their UHF antenna causing a delay in the transmission of the previously recorded message.

Another unsolved mystery is the transmission's point of origin. Data from TDRS indicated the message was broadcast from an empty sector of space, 297 million miles from Earth...232 million miles from *Cetus Prime*'s last reported position.

Subsequent attempts to contact the vessel were unsuccessful, and no further transmissions from the doomed ship were ever received. NASA ceased monitoring all deep space radio bands for messages from *Cetus Prime* on the one-year anniversary of its last transmission.

As the mission had been classified as a DoD Special Access Program black operation, the families of the *Cetus Prime* crew never knew their loved ones had traveled into space. Instead, the crew had been instructed to tell their families they had volunteered to participate in a special, eighteen-month training assignment to simulate the isolation effects of deep space travel, occupying a mocked-up spaceship at an undisclosed NASA facility.

In March 1996, NASA informed the families that a tragic accident had taken the lives of their loved ones. The families were told the helicopter returning the astronauts home at the end of their training mission had disappeared over the Pacific Ocean. After an exhaustive search, the helicopter and its occupants were declared lost at sea.

Paul Morgan kept his button with the pictures of Avery Lockett, Nick Reed and Christine Baker. To this day, on the anniversary of their last transmission, Morgan pins on the button and travels to Arlington National Cemetery to place flowers at the feet of the tombstones marking their empty graves.

So ends *UMO*. Fast forward twenty-three years. The opening chapter of *Skywave*, book one of the Rorschach Explorer Missions series, begins on the next page.

ALL HAIL 3LROY

Kiera Walsh clicked the hyperlink embedded in the text message and waited for her tablet to connect to the podcast. During the wait, she stared out at the ocean and mumbled, "I can't believe I got suckered into doing this."

The site took a full minute to load, providing Kiera enough time to lay her tablet on the balcony table and head inside for another glass of iced tea. When she returned outside, she set the glass down next to her tablet, catching a glimpse of the podcast home page. She lifted the tablet to take a closer look and began to laugh. "Oh, my God. Unbelievable."

The center of the screen was dominated by the frozen video image of a scraggly-bearded man wearing a paper crown from a popular burger chain. The crown was cocked to the side of his head, presumably to reinforce the "gangsta" vibe apparent on the rest of the page. Kiera assumed the man in the video was none other than the channel's host, "hizz boi 3lr0y," as she noticed the T-shirt he wore depicted the sixties cartoon character, Elroy.

Below the video was a caption that read, "Dey keep throwin shade, but 3lr0y unswayed!" Kiera laughed again. "Ah, our boy Elroy is a gangsta *and* a poet. How awful! No wonder NASA shot him down."

Her opinion of 3lr0y, a.k.a. Ajay Joshi, didn't improve as she scanned the rest of the site. The right sidebar provided thumbnail images of other recent video diatribes, each displaying captions with cringe-worthy, rap-inspired rhymes. Beneath the center-screen feature video, there was a section titled "Da truf is 0ut der!" It contained links to recent "news" articles about UFO sightings, alien conspiracies and the like.

But the most hilarious section ran down the left-hand sidebar. Here, 3lr0y had created a pithy bio that was more of a dating-site profile than a listing of his bona fides, with categories such as favorite places to stargaze, best sci-fi flicks and hottest superhero vixens. For turn-ons, he listed "all thangs Jupiter," while he limited his turn-offs to "suck hole non-believers." This latter category had accumulated over five hundred thumbs-up votes. For grins, Kiera clicked on the vote tally to view the list of 3lr0y's like-minded visitors. As expected, the avatars and usernames revealed his followers to be a collection of anti-establishment, aliens-are-among-us fanatics.

Kiera hadn't paid attention to the vote totals below 3lr0y's videos when she first scanned the page, so she scrolled up to check out the stats. She was surprised to see that several of them had over a thousand views, each with hundreds of thumbs-up votes. While perusing the tallies, she noticed a flashing banner at the top of the page. It hadn't been there when the site initially loaded, so she presumed 3lr0y was in the midst of updating the site. The banner read, "Stay tuned, dawgs and bitches…New pruf coming 2m0rr0w!"

"Okay, I've seen enough," Kiera said as she closed the tablet's web browser. Opening her text app, she clicked on the message from Sarah and typed, "K. Looked at the link as promised."

To Kiera's dismay, Sarah replied within seconds. "So… what do u think? Can u help AJ?"

"AJ needs help all right, but not from me!" Kiera typed back. She included an emoticon of a tongue-drooping, cross-eyed smiley face.

"Yeah…I know. He's wacky, but he's really sweet," Sarah answered. There was a pause and then Sarah followed up with another text. "And he's really bummed out. Won't you please meet with him?"

"I'm an aerospace engineer, not a shrink," Kiera responded.

"I know, but you're the best AE I know!" came Sarah's swift reply. Attached to the text were several wide-smile emoticons.

"Um…I'm the only AE you know."

"PLEEEAAASSEEE!!! I'm on my knees begging."

Kiera sighed and rattled off her response. "Look, I get one week off a month. I'm not devoting a second of it to meet with a crude, misogynistic nutjob...no offense."

For several minutes, there was no response from Sarah. Kiera hated to be so blunt about it, but there was no way she was going to waste her time listening to 3lr0y's wacked-out theory about aliens on Callisto broadcasting radio greetings to Earth. The dude was an accountant, not a scientist. And he had zero experience analyzing radio signals. He was just an amateur astronomer with a home-made radio telescope in his backyard who'd watched a few too many *Star Trek* reruns as a child.

Kiera lowered the tablet to her lap and reached for her iced tea. In midgulp, she felt a buzz from the device. Sarah had written back. With another sigh, this one deeper, Kiera pressed her thumb on the lock-screen button to view the text.

"Didn't want to do this...but u leave me no choice. Meet with AJ or suffer the consequences," read Sarah's message. A second text followed close behind, accompanied by a winking smiley face. "I still have the video, u know...the FULL, UNCENSORED version."

"You wouldn't dare!" Kiera responded.

"Watch me, twinkle toes."

Friends shouldn't let friends record karaoke performances, Kiera thought. Ever. Especially when alcohol is involved. Doubly so when the staggering, off-key rendition includes a raunchy striptease and pole dance. While Kiera doubted Sarah was serious about posting the video, she knew her old roommate would continue to pester her until she got what she wanted. The threatened revenge porn was just Sarah's way of short-circuiting the pestering process.

"Fine. 30 minutes, no more," Kiera replied.

"Yay! He'll be in Cocoa day after tomorrow," came Sarah's immediate reply. "I gave him ur # yesterday. He'll contact u to arrange time & place."

"You did what?!!!"

"Kisses," said Sarah's final text.

Kiera searched her emoticon menu for the one depicting a middle-finger salute. She fired off a reply filled with two rows of the icon. Unsatisfied, Kiera blurted a stream of expletives loud enough to catch the attention of a woman and child walking along the surf a hundred yards in the distance. The sour-faced woman glared up at Kiera's fourth-floor balcony and shook her head. Red-faced, Kiera waved and shouted out an apology. When the woman was out of view, Kiera said, "Great way to start the vacay."

Later in the evening, with her takeout dinner of egg rolls and Szechuan chicken consumed, Kiera sat in the corner of her living room sofa with a half-empty glass of Chardonnay. On her lap rested her tablet, and once again she found herself gazing at Ajay Joshi's podcast channel.

Whether driven by curiosity or sadism, Kiera had resolved to view his videos before calling it a night, and now it was time to make her first selection.

There were a dozen videos available on the home page and an archive link to thirty others. As Kiera scanned the lyrical captions of the twelve main clips, it was apparent that most were devoted to Ajay's obsession with his supposed discovery of alien radio signals and his frustration with NASA and other "suck hole non-believers" who ignored his "pruf."

Among these clips, his featured video appeared to be the most recent, so she opted to start there and work backward in time. Before pressing play, Kiera whisked down the remainder of her wine and set the glass aside.

The video began with a dark screen and the sound of ocean waves. After several seconds, the waves soundtrack faded and a voice said, "Greetings, playas…It is, I, Elroy, come to drop mo' fo-one-one on yo sorry asses."

The dark screen began to lighten, revealing a blur of changing shapes and colors. As the camera's focus adjusted, Ajay appeared. Seated before the webcam, arms crossed like a posing hip-hop star, he had a scowl on his face and the burger-joint crown on his head.

Kiera winced, wondering if Ajay realized how comical his tough-guy presentation came across. The dark-skinned Nepali was string-bean thin, with biceps that looked like broomsticks poking out from the drooping sleeves of his Elroy T-shirt. Hardly the stuff of gangstas, she thought.

The laughable quality of the video was further bolstered by Ajay's speech pattern. His attempt to mesh contemporary American urban slang with the high-toned inflections common among East Indian cultures only exacerbated the goofiness of his delivery...all this before he dropped a morsel of "fo-one-one."

He held up a piece of paper and shook it at the camera. "Another diss from the naysayers!"

A subtitle appeared on the screen to clarify for his audience the identity of the antagonists who'd disrespected Ajay. The subtitle read, "Down wit NASAyerz."

"Good lord," Kiera said. "This might call for another glass of wine."

The early part of Ajay's rant focused on a letter he'd received from a NASA "scrub" on the day the video was shot. The bottom-feeding lackey, as Ajay also labeled him, had dared to challenge Ajay's interpretation of intermittent clicks on a recording of radio waves from Jupiter.

This injustice, Ajay explained, was the latest evidence of a massive cover-up to hide the presence of aliens on Jupiter's outermost moon, Callisto. Several groups within NASA had rejected his theory. Ajay reminded his viewers that scrubs from the European Space Agency, the Japanese Aerospace Exploration Agency, the China National Space Administration and the Russian space agency, Roscosmos, hadn't even bothered to respond to his emails.

While he railed against their collective ignorance, Kiera noticed Ajay's language and demeanor begin to change.

The angrier he became, the more forceful his delivery. There was authority in his voice. Aided by the discard of his crown, Ajay morphed from slapstick foil into impassioned crusader.

"They say the clicks come from Earthbound interference. Skywaves, they call them. Ionosondes," he said, using his fingers to form air-quotes around the two technical terms. "Well, I say, ionosondes, my ass!"

His expression was stern as he rattled off his rebuttal. "The sounds are clicks. They are not chirps. They are not lightning-induced static. They were recorded over a year-and-a-half period, by different Radio JOVE contributors in six different states, and the clicks occur *only* when Callisto passes in front of Io and Jupiter. The clicks make the same exact sounds in the same exact pattern, in exactly three-minute intervals, on all six recordings.

"Are we to believe that skywaves are capable of bouncing off the ionosphere with such precision, and that they inherently know to invade Io-B recordings when Callisto transits Jupiter?

"Some of the scrubs claim the clicks are electrical interference from appliances, or shortwave radio pranksters tapping out Morse code. Really? Are we to believe that the exact same type of appliance resides near the six different radio telescopes that have picked up the clicks? Hmmm? And that these appliances are turned on and off at precisely the same interval, producing identical click patterns? Or that a devious prankster travels around the country, perfectly guessing which Radio JOVE contributors will be recording Io-B storms on nights when Callisto, Io, Jupiter and Earth all line up, and *only* on those nights? This devious prankster is apparently so clever, he is able to then set up his radio near the contributors' telescopes and insert Morse-like, repeating signals?"

Kiera paused the recording as Ajay rose from his chair to emphasize his next point. She stood herself and headed for the kitchen. "Yep, more wine is definitely in order."

As she poured the Chardonnay, she considered Ajay's points. Although he was oversimplifying the explanations provided by his space agency villains, she had to admit his rebuttals contained rational challenges. Whether they were accurate or not was another matter, but at least he appeared to have counterarguments that weren't based on comic book gibberish.

On her way back to the living room sofa, she made a mental note to learn more about Radio JOVE before meeting Ajay. She'd heard of the NASA program before and knew it was created to investigate magnetic storms on Jupiter, but that was the extent of her knowledge.

Seated before the tablet again, Kiera unpaused the video. Ajay, now in full meltdown, walked about the room, shouting, "No! I say no! And no, again! The signals come from Callisto, not Earth. They are being purposely broadcast by an intelligent life-form. They are not ionosondes, on Earth, Io, Callisto or Jupiter! It is an alien greeting. Or a distress call. I don't know which, but I do know this: I will *not* be silenced!"

Out of breath, Ajay slumped back in his chair and glared at the camera. He planted the crown back on top of his thick, black hair with defiance chiseled on his face. As his respiration settled down, he flashed a gang sign and said, "'Til next time, peace out, bros and bitches!"

Fade to black.

ABOUT THE AUTHOR

Kevin Patrick Donoghue is the author of the Anlon Cully Chronicles archaeology mystery series, the Rorschach Explorer Missions science fiction series and the Unity of Four medical thriller series. His books include:

THE ANLON CULLY CHRONICLES SERIES:

Book 1: *Shadows of the Stone Benders*
Book 2: *Race for the Flash Stone*
Book 3: *Curse of the Painted Lady*
Book 4: *Priestess of Paracas*

THE RORSCHACH EXPLORER MISSIONS SERIES:

Prequel: *UMO* (novella)
Book 1: *Skywave*
Book 2: *Magwave*
Book 3: *Dynewave*

THE UNITY OF FOUR SERIES:

Book 1: *The GODD Chip*

Ways to stay in touch with the author: follow K. Patrick Donoghue — Novelist on Facebook or join the author's email subscriber list by visiting kpatrickdonoghue.com and clicking on the "Join Email List" link on main menu.

Made in the USA
Middletown, DE
16 July 2023

35288856R00076